THE DAKOTA DEAL

Escaped prisoner John McCallam's discovery of a deserted cabin and a dead body provides an opportunity to assume a new identity, and different clothing. But McCallam doesn't know the nature of the man he's become. The people of North Bend mistake McCallam for the notorious gunman, Frank Chater, hired to rid the town of the growing menace of Royce Chisholm and his sadistic sidekicks. Has he exchanged one prison for another? Or can he escape both?

DAN CLAYMAKER

THE DAKOTA DEAL

Complete and Unabridged

LINFORD
Leicester

First published in Great Britain in 2008 by
Robert Hale Limited
London

First Linford Edition
published 2009
by arrangement with
Robert Hale Limited
London

British Library CIP Data

Claymaker, Dan.
    The Dakota deal - - (Linford western library)
    1. Western stories
    2. Large type books
    I. Title II. Series
    823.9′14–dc22

    ISBN 978–1–84782–697–8

Published by
F. A. Thorpe (Publishing)
Anstey, Leicestershire

Set by Words & Graphics Ltd.
Anstey, Leicestershire
Printed and bound in Great Britain by
T. J. International Ltd., Padstow, Cornwall

This book is printed on acid-free paper

This one for *M* with fond regard

1

John McCallam crossed the border into North Dakota and reached the snow-line an hour before sunset.

His priority then was shelter for the night; somewhere dry, warm, out of the whipping winter wind, and as deep into the pine forest as he could get. The deeper the better. That, too, was a priority when you were an escaped prisoner three days on the run from the penitentiary at Williamsville.

He reined the stolen mount to a halt and patted the mare's neck. 'Good to be free, eh, gal?' he murmured, permitting himself a soft smile as he recalled how he had taken the horse, one of the guards' special mounts saddled and ready to ride, from under their very noses on the chill grey dawn of an overcast day. The mare, he thought, had seemed almost grateful to have a new owner.

The man grunted as he turned the collar of his coat high into his neck and took in his surroundings. Snow and dense forest ahead of him; thickening cloud threatening more snow to the east; a fast sinking sun to the west, and to the south . . . He preferred not to look. He had escaped the south, left it and five years of his life behind him in the squalor of the pen on a trumped-up charge of his complicity in the Raines Ridge bank raid. Now he was free — almost.

He gave the mare a final pat and clicked his tongue for her to walk on. The forest shadows waited like a welcoming mantle.

★   ★   ★

It was close on another hour, with the night gathering fast around him when McCallam eased the mount into a snow-covered clearing and saw the dark bulk of the cabin at the far edge of it.

A door, window, small porch with a sinking, lopsided roof, leaning stack; no sign of life, no movement, no sound. A trapper's cabin, he wondered? Abandoned, or vacated temporarily?

McCallam sat the mount in silence and simply watched, his gaze flat and steady, his breath drifting on the pinched night air. Watching had become an art he had perfected. He could watch for hours without moving; watch the gaolers come and go about their ritual duties, until their every steps, every gesture, sound and words he could see and hear long after they had left and taken the light with them.

Cloud scudded high above the heads of the pines and parted to reveal the mellow stare of the moon. McCallam grunted softly to himself, fondled the mount's ears and patted its head. 'Let's go see,' he murmured, and walked the horse on.

He reined back in the shadow of the shack to the left of the door, dismounted, hitched the mount to the porch post, and moved quietly to the dusty, grime-smeared window. He cupped his hands to his eyes and peered inside. Shapes, but too dark and vague to be recognized. He waited, listening, standing back from the window now to watch the door before approaching.

It opened with a scratching scrape and protesting creak to his touch. He sniffed. Stale smoke, a hint of recent cooking. McCallam waited for his eyes to adjust to the gloom. Table, chair, plates, tin mugs, a skinning knife, stewpot, long-handled wooden spoon; assorted cloths, drawstring tobacco pouch, charred pipe.

McCallam blinked. A half-empty bottle of whiskey. 'Hell,' he hissed, stepping aside instinctively from the open door. Seemed like the place had not been abandoned. Fellow living here could be back anytime, specially with the night closing in. Maybe it was time to move on, help himself to any scraps of food, take a swig of that whiskey . . .

He hesitated. There was another door

4

ahead of him. A bunkroom? Sure to be, and that meant blankets. If he was going to spend a winter's night in the shelter of whatever scrub and brush he could find, blankets would be vital against the weather coming in. He stepped quickly across the room.

Again he waited, watching, listening, his nerve ends alive to the slightest sound, the softest movement. Nothing. Only silence. His hand dropped to the latch, lifted it and let the door swing open. It moved slowly as if unused to intrusion and squeaked tiredly on its hinges.

It must have been a full minute before his eyes pierced the intense darkness of the small room. He saw a window, a stool, the bunk, a pile of blankets heaped together like sleeping hunchbacks, and the unmistakable mound of a body sprawled across the floor.

Very stiff and very dead.

2

The snowfall had deepened round the cabin and wrapped the tree boughs in white scarves by the time McCallam had found a lantern, primed and lit it, persuaded wet logs to burn in the grate, bedded down the mount with warm blankets and feed in the lean-to out back and finally closed the door on the night.

He had yet to examine the dead body.

He poured a long measure of the whiskey into a tin mug, rummaged until he found some still edible jerky and stood with his back to the now crackling fire.

The dead man, he reckoned, had been no trapper, no prospector either. Just a fellow passing through, or here for a meeting that had turned fatally nasty? He appeared not to have been robbed. The cabin had not been trashed or ransacked. Nothing seemed to be very obviously missing.

The fellow had been shot through the back of the head, probably on his knees, execution-style. And his killer, or killers, had simply closed the door, taken the man's horse, and ridden on. A murder without a motive. Or so it seemed.

Five years in the pen had taught McCallam that rarely did a fellow die without reason, unless caught in the cross-fire of others. No, he figured, somebody had purposely trailed out here to the forest, maybe crossed the border same as he had — the difference being that the killer knew of the cabin and that his target would be waiting here.

An argument; a disagreement; a revenge killing? Who could say? But the body might reveal something.

Very little as it happened, save for the tightly folded paper found in the dead man's shirt pocket. McCallam studied it carefully. It was a wire sent out of the town of Markfield to the telegraph office in Williamsville, addressed to one Frank Chater, and read: BE NORTH BEND SOONEST. DEAL ON. It was signed Henry Begine. 'So,' murmured McCallam, 'now you have a name.'

But who was Frank Chater? What had he done for a living? Was he a drifter, a loner, perhaps a roughneck gunslinger, a wanted man on the run much like himself, or just a simple living, ordinary fellow, the sort you might meet in any bar in any street, in any town? He doubted the ordinariness of this man. He squatted closer to the body to examine the man's features. Death had already taken its toll, reducing what had once been a tanned, almost swarthy skin to a grey mask that looked as if it had been sprinkled with fine creek dust. But the set of the chin, the straight nose, hooded eyes, firm mouth confirmed a man of decision and purpose. No drifter, no loser, but he might well have been a loner.

McCallam peered at the man's well-kept hands, clean fingernails, no calluses. A gambling man, more used to dealing from a freshly cut deck than wielding an axe? Or maybe a lawman? There was no star, but the fellow's clothes and boots were quality, specially the tailored buckskin jacket. Lawman style. A marshal perhaps. And that holstered piece on the gunbelt was no cheap second-hand Colt. That, he knew, was a tooled piece a man could rely on.

But why had he not drawn it? Had he made no attempt to defend himself against his killer? Had there been no time? Or had he known and trusted his visitor? Who was Henry Begine, and what was the North Bend deal?

McCallam moved back to the warmth of the fire, poured himself another measure and began to let his thoughts range freely over the wild plan that was beginning to take shape in his mind.

Supposing he were to become Frank Chater?

If he was going to make good his

meticulously planned escape from Williamsville and stay free he needed a fresh identity. Maybe it was time to bury John McCallam. After all, it was a certainty that lawmen out of Williamsville had taken up the chase by now to recapture him. They might be close, simply waiting on the weather to clear before swooping in, a full posse giving no quarter. The sooner he was further north the more comfortable he would feel, more so if he had become another man.

Would it work; might he get away with posing as Frank Chater?

But how well known was the fellow? How many hereabouts in this part of North Dakota knew him, had met him, maybe ridden with him?

He closed his mind to the questions; he was creating difficulties for himself, imagining situations that might never happen. If he was going to assume Chater's identity, now was the time to do it. He had some hours still to his advantage.

McCallam finished the measure of whiskey and set to work.

★   ★   ★

The snowfall had drifted south and the heavy skies thinned to a hint of dawn, the long night already passed and the wind eased to catch its breath.

In the forest cabin, McCallam dimmed the lantern glow until it faded and stood to his full height in the dead man's boots. They were a surprisingly good fit. He stamped his feet to let his toes stretch and settle, then walked a few paces round the room. The boots would do fine, as would the rest of the man's outfit: his shirt, pants and, not least, the buckskin jacket that might have been tailored for him.

He grunted, but inwardly stifled an icy shudder. He had never stood in a dead man's boots before, never stripped a dead body of its clothes and set to wearing them himself. It was an unnatural sensation, like slithering out

11

of an old skin into a something not quite new.

He placed Chater's hat on his head, pulled at the brim, adjusted it, smoothed it, touched it again and walked to the snow-pocked window. Did he feel like Frank Chater? Could a change of clothes do that to a fellow? But how could he feel like the man? He had never known him. One thing was for sure, he certainly did not feel like the John McCallam who had found the cabin only a few hours back. That fellow had somehow faded into a dark past. So maybe he was Chater's ghost.

He stifled another icy shudder but had no difficulty strapping on the dead man's gunbelt. The Colt seemed to rest natural at his side. Damnit, it might have been made for him personally, just like the jacket.

He waited a moment, legs apart, feeling for his balance, then, with one swift flash of his hand drew the piece and steadied it.

Been a long time, he mused, holding

the stance, his eyes unblinking, staring, the weight of the gun steady in his grip, the soft chill and smoothness of the bone butt a familiar sensation. It had been a long time ago, back in those days when John McCallam had been — He broke the reverie, checked that the Colt was loaded, and holstered it.

The first light of the day fingered the window with all the silence of what might have been a real ghost.

* * *

An hour later, the man closed the cabin door on the dead body and stood for a moment taking in the colder, sharper air, the brighter light as day began to grow, and reflected quietly that he had also closed a door on the life of John McCallam.

He was leaving him behind; the escaped prisoner was now no more than a bundle of old clothes he would bury somewhere in the forest. Soon, perhaps in a matter of only a few hours, somebody would reach the cabin, find the body stripped to only worn johns, and wonder why. But by then, Frank Chater would be miles to the north, trailing his way through the dense forest that would not thin until he reached the foothills of the mountain ranges.

Once there, he would simply disappear until he judged it safe to assume that the weather had got the better of any following party and they had turned back.

He had made good progress through the lighter snow-fall of a track under the protective shelter of the pine boughs when he heard the shout and two shots up ahead.

He reined back sharply, steadied the mare, waited a moment, his eyes narrowing on the gloom of the forest, then slid quietly from the saddle. 'Easy, gal, easy,' he murmured, hitching the mount on a loose rein. He waited again, listening, watching. Silence. Nothing moving. But there had been a shout and there had been shots.

He patted the mare's neck and moved away, creeping softly through the snow, the Colt steady in his grip. Still no sound, still no movement. He passed into the tighter cover of a thicker pine, waited, listened, conscious of his breath drifting like white wings without a body.

And then he saw the shapes only yards ahead.

3

There were two men. The fellow to the left was stocky, heavy-chested, broad-shouldered with a soft battered hat pulled low over his ears. His partner was taller, leaner, his limbs loose and easy, his long, rat's-tail hair frozen like grey ice across his shoulders. Both men wore layers of thick fur skins secured at the waist by a length of rope; their legs were lost in patched pants and knee-high boots, their hands tight on rifles. Their mounts and a loaded pack horse were hitched some distance away.

Mountain men, hunters, trappers, or rough drifters down on their luck and looking for ready pickings, wondered McCallam, pressing a shoulder into the pine trunk as he watched? He flexed his fingers across the butt of the Colt. Scumbags which ever way you looked at them, he decided.

16

The men's attention concentrated on the older, white-haired man sprawled in the snow in front of them, his hands gripping his blood-soaked thigh, his low moans flushing a thickening cloud of breath round his head.

'Sonofa-goddamn-bitch,' croaked the old man. 'What the hell you wanna . . .' He grimaced and gripped the thigh tighter, then spat. 'Damnit, why don't you get to shootin' straighter if you're goin' to —'

'Shut up,' growled the heavy-chested fellow, prodding his rifle threateningly. 'What's your name? Where'd you come from?'

'Go to hell!' snapped the old man, his eyes burning in his weathered, wind-strafed head. 'I wouldn't give you —'

The leaner man kicked snow into the old fellow's face. 'A sour-tongued has-been,' he sneered. 'Take his boots, anythin' else of use, and his horse, then finish him. We ain't got the time for chat.' He lifted his gaze to the tree-tops and the gathering menace of snow clouds. 'Weather's closin' in.'

The stocky man pulled at the brim of his hat. 'Be a pleasure,' he chuckled. 'A real pleasure.'

The old man grimaced again and squirmed, smearing blood across the snow until it lay like a spilled sunset. He tried to lift himself, his sweat dripping freely through his days' old stubble. 'Go ahead, rat,' he croaked, 'if that's the best you can do.' He glared at the man with the levelled rifle as if defying him to close his pressure on the trigger. 'Well, what you waitin' for? I ain't goin' no place. Can't make this any easier for you, can I?'

The stocky man sneered, raised the rifle a fraction higher and might well have applied that fatal pressure had the snow at his feet not erupted as two shots blazed and echoed like clattering birds.

The stocky man swung round, the rifle lowered to his waist in a tightened grip. The leaner man, checking the load of the pack horse, flung himself to his left, retained his balance and grabbed his own rifle from its scabbard. The old man's eyes widened in his head and did not blink.

The Colt roared a third shot that blazed into the stocky man's head, throwing him back to the snow where he lay like a large black bear.

The leaner man had watched, bewildered, at the sight of the shooting of his partner and could only continue to stare as a figure in a buckskin jacket stood clear of his cover in the pines, waited a moment and then, without a murmur, fired a fourth shot which the lean man knew was about to end his day before the real light had broken.

The echo of the shot climbed and drifted into the silence of a fresh snowfall. The man with the Colt stood perfectly still, his gaze steady as if looking into a past long forgotten until now. The snowfall thickened. The old man blinked and found the breath at last to murmur, 'Damn my eyes if that ain't Frank Chater!'

★　★　★

'Knew it, just knew it, minute you stepped clear of them pines. Cupcake, I says to m'self, Cupcake — that bein' my name — your searchin' is over. You've found him! Right here in front of your very eyes — Frank Chater, large as life and twice as welcome, seein' as how I was in somethin' of a predicament at that moment with them loused-up, thievin' drifters all set to take what they could of an old fella and to hell with it. Or so they thought, eh, mister, till you stepped in.

'And that's when I knew, saw that buckskin jacket just like I'd been told to watch for, and that hat. But when you fired that piece, when you did that . . . oh, yes, I knew then for sure that here was Frank Chater. Ain't nobody, not nobody, handles a Colt like Frank Chater. Everybody knows that, m'self included, not that I'd clapped eyes on you till today. But, it's like Mr Begine said, 'You'll know him sure enough when you see him.' And he was right. Dead right. He's our wealthy storekeeper, by the way.

'Say, I'm gettin' ahead of m'self when I should be thankin' you, mister — really thankin' you, full to the brim — for savin' my life. And you did just that, make no mistake. You bet. But that ain't the point, is it? Nossir, not the point at all.'

The old man's voice had droned on tirelessly for some minutes while McCallam did his best to clean up the wounded thigh, bind and strap it and ease the fellow from the open ground to a safer, drier area beneath the overhang of a pine bough. He had worked in a haze of the man's words spilling like splintering ice from his mouth and the chilling realization that he had been taken to be Frank Chater on sight. There had been no hesitation, no question in Cupcake's mind. The coat, the hat and, to settle it beyond doubt, the shooting of the bushwhackers had sealed it.

Frank Chater had been a man of some reputation, McCallam mused, not least because of his prowess as a gunslinger. That was worrying, but a deeper worry was the dilemma of the situation he had ridden into: did he own up to being John McCallam and tell the old man what he had found at the cabin, or did he remain Frank Chater?

Cupcake's voice droned on. 'The point is, I've found you, and that's a relief, believe me. Four days out of North Bend and not a sight of you and, darn me, not much hope of one neither when I bunked up best I could close to that old nag of mine last night. Gettin' to think I'd missed you. But how, damn it? Mr Begine was certain as how you'd be trailin' this way out of Williamsville. 'My guess would be', he'd said, 'that Chater will head north on the forest trail. That way he'll stay clear of probin' eyes and curious drifters who might just get smart enough to go blabbin' that a fast gun is headin' for North Bend. He wouldn't want that, not Frank Chater. T'ain't the way he operates'. And you sure as hell wouldn't, would you, mister?'

The old man's wet, tired eyes had stared pleadingly into McCallam's face.

'Sure,' McCallam heard himself saying. 'That's right. The forest trail. Made good sense.'

The man's face relaxed to a beaming smile. 'Knew it, damn it! That's what I said to m'self last night curled up there in that perishin' snow. Forest trail makes sense, I said. Said it out loud. Must've been heard, eh, Mr Chater? Good Lord up there had his window open and he heard me!'

McCallam grunted and squatted closer to peer at the strapped thigh where a dark stain of blood was already spreading.

'You're losin' a lot of blood, fella. You need a doc. I figure there's lead in there.'

Cupcake winced. 'Don't you fret none, Mr Chater. Old Doc Tucker back

23

in North Bend will fix it fine. He's got fingers that work magic. Bit of scumbag lead in a wound — bah, it won't trouble him none! He'll have that blade of his out faster than a fella can blink, and before you know it . . . ' A rush of pain through the leg drowned Cupcake's words in a groan.

McCallam stood to his full height, drew the collar of the buckskin coat high into his neck and narrowed his gaze on the thickening snowfall through the pine boughs.

'This weather's closin' fast. We'd best settle for an hour or so. No point in trailin' through blizzard.'

'You bet,' said Cupcake, tightening his two-handed grip on the upper part of his thigh. It'll mebbe ease in an hour or so, then we can move. And don't you get to thinkin' we'll need to travel slow on my account, mister. No chance. The need for you to be in North Bend is a whole sight greater than mine. We've got a town back there goin' to the dogs of hell — and fast — so my leg here don't count for a bag of beans. Soon as we're able we'll ride, and no stoppin' till we hit North Bend. Agreed?'

Now was the time to break the news to the old man, thought McCallam. To tell him who he was, where he had come from, what he had found at the cabin; that he was not Frank Chater, never had been Frank Chater and never could be or wanted to be. He was John McCallam, an escaped prisoner on the run — and desperate to stay free.

'Best time we can hope to make to North Bend is two days, weather permittin'.' Cupcake blinked, ran a hand over his eyes and tucked the bulk of a scarf into his neck. 'Be an idea to help ourselves to them skins the scumbags got packed on that horse there. Stayin' warm's a priority, eh, mister? Keep that gun hand of yours warm, eh?' He winked. 'Worth its weight in gold, I'll bet.'

'Look,' began McCallam, 'there's somethin' you should — '

'I'll say no more, Mr Chater,' said

25

Cupcake, raising a hand. 'I understand. Man of your callin' needs to keep himself to himself. I figure that. Understand it. Your line of work is a dedication. Said that all along, ever since our town committee agreed as how we should seek the services of a professional and Henry Begine said he knew how to contact you — a real-life, dedicated gunman with a natural feel for justice. And that man's Frank Chater.' He winked again. 'Ain't no other way North Bend's ever goin' to rid itself of that scurvy rat, Chisholm. We all said it, every last man thinkin' and speakin' as one: only man who's ever goin' to kill Royce Chisholm is Frank Chater. And you'll do that for us, do it for North Bend, won't you, mister?'

4

McCallam did not rest. He sat hunched in the snow, wrapped in skins, his hat pulled low over his eyes to afford no more than a narrow sighting of the old man cocooned in his own nest of blankets and furs. The horses, now totalling five, had been hitched in the deepest of the pine cover; the bodies of the drifters left where they had fallen.

Within a half-hour of settling to see out the blizzard, the silence had closed in and tightened, as if a door on the pine forest world had been locked and bolted. There was nothing to do save sit and wait.

It had taken some time to sift thoughts of the pen, the cabin and the drifters to one side and to concentrate on the immediate problem: Just how in hell was he going to avoid ever setting foot in North Bend? He felt he had no choice but to help the old man best he could; at least deliver him safely into the hands of a doctor. So maybe he could stay with Cupcake to within, say, a mile of the town, then tell him the truth, explain how the mistake had come about, and ride on.

But supposing . . .

Supposing a posse had ridden out of Williamsville in pursuit of him; how far away were they? Would the weather turn them back? Supposing they reached the cabin and found the body stripped of its clothing. Might they deduce that McCallam was attempting to assume a new identity? Might one of the posse recognize the dead man as Frank Chater?

Perhaps stumbling across that particular body had been a bad deal from the pack for McCallam. Of all the dead men he might have found, he had to find Chater, a killer for hire!

But why all the urgency to get him to North Bend? Why had the old man been sent to find him? And just who was Royce Chisholm?

The questions were still burning holes through McCallam's thoughts when the blizzard finally eased, the old man stirred and plans were made to trail steadily northwards.

'We loose-line the spare mounts and get you and that dead leg fixed tight to your horse,' McCallam had ordered. 'No shiftin', and you hold to my pace. Understand? Any gettin' ahead in these conditions with you as you are and we're askin' for trouble.

'If all goes well and the weather holds in our favour, we'll mebbe hole-up late afternoon and light a fire. I gotta get clean strappin' on that leg or you'll lose it. Is that something else you understand?'

'Yessir!' Cupcake had beamed with a compliance that lit a twinkle in his eyes. 'Say this for you, Mr Chater, you sure know how to get organized. You bet. Still, I guess that's another sign of the dedicated gunman: bein' organized. Got to have a plan, ain't you? Can't just go into things piecemeal and scratch-bitty, can you? Nossir! Organization, that's the key, just like Jess Hart said.'

'Hart?' queried McCallam.

'Sheriff Hart,' said Cupcake. 'He's the law around North Bend. Well, tries to be when Chisholm'll let him — which ain't none too often by most reckonin'. Things ain't been the same for Jess since Chisholm shot his right-hand man, Ike Wallow.' The old man sighed. 'Poor devil.'

McCallam mounted up and clicked his tongue for the mare to walk on. 'Nice and easy here till we get to seein' how deep the snowfall. Might find ourselves havin' to track some distance west.'

'Whatever you say, Mr Chater,' Cupcake had grinned. 'You're the man in charge here. I'm just the fella who had the good fortune to find you!'

'Just why did you come lookin' for me in the first place?' McCallam asked.

'Ah,' said Cupcake, 'now that was Henry Begine's doin'. Oh, yes, and typical of him too. You see, we hadn't had no answer to the last wire we sent you, and things were gettin' mighty pressin' with Chisholm threatenin' to take Jess Hart's badge and pin it on himself, damn him. Then there was that shenanigan at the Saddles saloon where young Maisie Peach had flatly refused to . . . well, whatever it was Chisholm was demandin', and she and the other bar gals took to lockin' themselves in their rooms till Moses Fletcher — he owns the outfit — did somethin' about Chisholm's behaviour.'

'And did he?'

Cupcake spat into the snow. 'Did he hell as like! Nossir, he stood back while Chisholm and one of his henchmen kicked down the doors and took away the keys. Then they gave the gals a thrashin' and left poor old Maisie black and blue from head to toe. She ain't right yet.'

The old man spat again. 'Anyhow it was then that Mr Begine, Doc Tucker and the others figured as how you had to be found — and quick before North Bend gets to runnin' with blood. All we want, Mr Chater, is an end to Royce Chisholm. And for that we'll pay real handsome, just like we outlined in the deal.'

The deal, pondered McCallam, what had been the deal? Something big enough, tempting enough to bring a hired gun of Chater's status at least as far as the forest cabin on his way to North Bend. But what had happened in those four walls? Who had been his treacherous visitors? Men known to him, or simply hungry drifters?

Cupcake's voice was droning on again, but now as a diversion to himself against the throb of the wound.

'   . . . it's like I say, there's always somebody some place who steps forward to restore your faith in human nature — for whatever that's worth — and settle bad issues on the credit side. Said as much to Maisie Peach. Maisie, I says, darn me, if there won't come a day, when a fella will step out of the shadows and you'll know him to be the one who's your destiny. Same as it was for me, eh, Mr Chater, when you stepped out of them pines back there and blazed them two-bit dogs into oblivion . . . '

Cupcake was still talking when McCallam heard the first crack of twig somewhere to his left, followed by a second crack and a scuff of movement through the snow.

They had company, closing fast.

★ ★ ★

A chill gripped McCallam's stomach. He took a deep breath and slid the reins lightly through his fingers. Cupcake had fallen silent and suddenly watchful. He glanced quickly at McCallam and winked.

'I hear 'em,' he murmured. 'You got a fix?'

'To the left, workin' deep. Keepin' to our pace.'

'See anythin'?'

'Not yet.'

They moved on, the horses picking

their way through the snowfall to feel for each step, every lift and fall of the frozen ground. The trailed mounts followed silently in their wake, tossing their heads from time to time, snorting, but relieved it seemed to be moving against the biting cold.

Another crack of twig, more scuffing, this time closer.

'How many?' hissed Cupcake through the side of his mouth, his gaze held steadily ahead.

'Hard to say,' answered McCallam, risking a sideways glance into the shadowy depths of forest. 'Three. No less. Could be more.'

'You figure they know you?'

'I figure,' said McCallam, the chill in his stomach gripping tighter until it reached his backbone.

Williamsville men, he wondered? A posse of guards from the penitentiary? If so, they had ridden hard, but somehow bypassed or missed the cabin. Had they heard the shots that killed the drifters? Must have, he reckoned. Did they recognize him in his changed outfit? They would, specially if chief guard Bucks Slater was leading them. He could smell a prisoner at a quarter of a mile.

'Shall we try for a run?' hissed Cupcake again.

'Snow's too deep. Horses wouldn't hold this pace.'

'Kinda risky, ain't it?' grunted Cupcake. 'They could pick us off easy as poppin' plump turkeys.'

'I don't reckon them for wantin' us dead. They want live bodies.'

Cupcake pondered for a moment. 'Seems like you know these fellas pretty well.'

'If they're who I think they are, I know 'em like the back of my hand.'

Cupcake grinned softly. 'Comes of havin' a reputation, eh? Trouble round every corner. You bet! So how you goin' to handle this bunch, Mr Chater?'

McCallam let the question hang. Fact was, he had no idea how to handle whoever was trailing them. Had he been alone he might have risked a dash into deeper cover, but if he left the old man now, he would be dead within minutes. Cupcake was of no value. McCallam was an escaped prisoner on whom chief guard Slater and his side-kicks were going to wreak a painful retribution. Prisoners did not escape Slater's gaol. And if they did, they were always recaptured and brought back to Williamsville to suffer an even grimmer fate than before. McCallam knew. He had heard their screams in the night.

Cupcake began to whistle softly, the tone climbing as if in a haze to the high treetops.

'Kinda comforts my nerves,' he smiled, winking again. 'Settles the tension. You ever need to whistle, Mr Chater, or mebbe you don't have nerves, eh? Mebbe they're all tightened up in that stare. You should see yourself stare, mister. It's one helluvah — Hold it. I think trouble's finally surfaced.'

McCallam reined back sharply at the sight of chief guard Slater sitting his mount some forty yards down the barely discernible track, a Winchester held barrel high in his right hand.

'Figured I'd catch up with you sooner or later, McCallam. Took a little longer than I'd have preferred in this weather, but I'm a determined man, as you know well.' Slater spat, smiled, shifted to the stance of his mount and bunched the reins firmly in one hand.

McCallam sighed, the stream of white breath clouding round his head like a veil. He glanced quickly to his left, to the right, for a hint of Slater's men. Nothing. But how many were riding with him? How close were they? Within gunshot range? He caught a glimpse of the flushed, bemused expression on Cupcake's face. What must be reeling through the old man's thoughts? Even so, was that a wink or simply the sting of cold air?

Slater had eased his mount a step forward. 'Been a busy fella, it seems,' he leered, one eye half closing as if to burn into him. 'Robbed me of my best horse there; got yourself a new outfit — stolen, you can be sure — and committed one whole heap of a bloody shootin' back down the trail. Them poor hunters never stood a goddamn chance, I'll wager. So now you've stolen their horses along of mine.' He shook his head. 'My, my, McCallam, you're sure in some deep trouble here.'

He spat. 'Don't know who your partner is, but things ain't lookin' too rosy for him neither. Mebbe you'd just best get yourself down from that horse and drop the piece you got slung 'neath that fancy buckskin coat — which, from here, looks to be just my size.' He grinned and wiped the back of his hand across his mouth. 'Do it, damn your eyes!' he growled. 'Do it now, and then before I drag you back to Williamsville I'm goin' to thrash you to within an inch of your two-bit life.'

5

McCallam watched. He kept his gaze tight on Slater's face, particularly the eyes. He knew those eyes; of course he did. How many times had he seen them, fiery as hot coals, burning into him as he prepared for one of his sadistic knife-cutting, boot-kicking sessions? How many times . . . ?

But there had always been a weakness. Just as there was now.

That same impatience. 'Do it,' the man had ordered. 'Do it!' he would repeat, time and time again until it seemed like they were the only words echoing round the dark, dank, miserable walls of the pen.

And McCallam had simply watched.

'Get down!' ordered Slater again. 'Down f'Chris'sake.'

McCallam eased slowly, carefully from the saddle, smoothing a hand down the mare's neck as he went, whispering a soft reassurance to her, stroking an ear, taking all the time his churning stomach could muster to place a boot into snow.

But still watching.

He saw Slater twitch in his hold on the rifle. The first hint of impatience. He watched as the gaoler began to sweat, saw the beading bubble like crystals on his brow.

'Down, McCallam, down! I ain't sayin' it again, f'Chris'sake.'

Patience almost exhausted, thought McCallam.

Slater had only two choices: blaze that Winchester into a blood-swamping hole through McCallam's gut, or stand his ground, steady his nerves and try to control his impatience. Maybe he would do neither. Maybe he would hesitate just long enough to give McCallam the edge.

'Take that fancy jacket off,' ordered Slater.

And there it was — the fatal edge.

McCallam smiled softly to himself as he began to ease the jacket from his shoulders, free one arm, then let the natural drape of the garment fall across the freed hand.

That was the moment.

The hidden hand swept like a shaft of light to McCallam's holstered Colt, drew it and blazed two shots that flung Slater from his horse and thudded the body into the snow.

In the same instant, Cupcake's unsheathed rifle rained a hail of lead into the darker depths of the forest, the roar echoing across the snarl of McCallam's Colt.

The old man winced at the throb of the pain in his thigh, but remained in the saddle, his arms, hands and fingers working frantically but without pausing through the actions of firing.

McCallam squirmed through the snow on his stomach, seeking the body of the man he had just killed as the only cover to be had.

A scream echoed and then spun to a

miserable groan in the darkness of surrounding trees. A horse whinnied, a man shouted, hoofs pounded through snow, swirling it in ever thickening clouds. Another shout. More echoes as Cupcake's rifle continued to blaze.

McCallam was aware of a shape, a horse and rider, charging straight for him. He watched, waited, his breath tightening until the mount was almost upon him, then fired, felling the rider into a spin that landed him face down in the snow.

And then silence. An almost visible silence that might have been swished aside like a heavy drape.

Cupcake lowered his rifle, released a long stream of breath, licked his lips and, in spite of the agonizing throb from the wound, beamed a warm, broad smile.

'Ain't this just turnin' out to be one helluva day!' he called across the snow as he watched McCallam come to his feet from behind the dead body, retrieve the buckskin jacket, shake it and slip it on without a word.

'Knew it, damn it, just knew it. Minute I opened my old eyes back there, I said to m'self: Cupcake, I said, this is goin' to be one helluva day. Yessir! How about that, Mr Chater, didn't I just know it?'

★ ★ ★

'And before you say it, mister, before you even *think* it, I've figured the whole darned thing. You've been travellin' incog ... incog ... under another fella's name. Ain't that so? Course it is.'

Cupcake winked and tapped a finger on the side of his nose, steadied his mount and stared deep into McCallam's eyes.

'I got you, mister. You bet I have. I'd be happy to wager best part of what I own — t'ain't a deal, but every snitch of it worthy — that you got yourself into some almighty heap of trouble some place back on the trail, way beyond the border, and found it one dire bit necessary to change your identity. Right? You bet. So Frank Chater is suddenly some two-bit poke of a fella name of McCallam. Right? Right again, I'll bet. Then, o' course, one thing leads on to another. For example ... you steal another fella's horse, you take up by chance on the trail he would have taken and lo and sonofabitch behold, them scumbag, murderin' louse we've just cleared, catch up with you — entirely because of me, right? — and you're forced to a shoot-out.'

Cupcake paused, took a deep breath and smiled. 'Didn't do so bad for an old 'un, did I? What you reckon Mr Chater? I read you right? I figure so. Minute I saw you ease down from that mount, with that same stare in your eyes, I knew — just knew — you were goin' to draw under the cover of your jacket. And I was right! You did just that.'

McCallam took a deep breath and glared defiantly. The time had come. The time was now. 'There's somethin' you should know,' he began. 'I am not Frank Chater, have never been Frank Chater, and have no intention of becomin' him. So you can go on foolin' yourself for as long as you like, old man, but them's the facts. I am *not* Frank Chater. Got it? My name is John McCallam, an escaped prisoner on the run from the pen at Williamsville and that scumbag lyin' there and whoever else we managed to flush out were guards sittin' hot on my tail. All right? You hearin' me there, fella, loud and clear?'

Cupcake's face had drained of colour to a washed-out grey almost as flat as the snow skies, his expression dissolved to a blank in which his eyes were simply holes and his mouth hung open. He could only stare, feeling nothing of the wound or the biting cold.

'Well,' said McCallam, relaxing his glare, 'have I made myself clear?'

'Sure,' began Cupcake slowly, softly, the stare locked into his face. 'Sure. You bet. I got it clear as day, Mr Chater:

you've taken on this McCallam name to keep Royce Chisholm wonderin' just who the hell it is has ridden into town. He won't know no fella name of McCallam will he? But damn it, he'd be sure to have heard of Frank Chater.'

'No!' flared McCallam, clenching his fists. 'No, that is not what I'm sayin'. I've told you, I am not Frank Chater. How many more times do I have to say it?'

Cupcake's face came alive again with a new, broader smile that flooded the colour into his cheeks. 'Tell you somethin', Mr Chater, you carry on bein' as insistent as you are that you're this fella McCallam, and you'll convince anybody. And your secret's safe with me. I won't say a word.'

McCallam sighed into a deep groan as his shoulders slumped despairingly. 'Goddamnit,' he hissed under his breath before kicking angrily into a drift of soft snow. 'Goddamnit!'

* * *

They trailed on in silence. Cupcake settled to the saddle and the gentle roll of the pace without too much discomfort. He whistled softly — annoyingly to McCallam's ears — pausing only to let a smug, satisfied grin break the pursed lips. He glanced from time to time at McCallam, but said nothing. The occasional wink seemed to sum up his thoughts without the need for words.

McCallam's mood and desperation deepened. He had got himself into this mess, he mused. It had been nothing but his own lack of resolve and weakness that had brought the old man to the point that no matter what McCallam said, however loudly he protested, or even raged against the fellow's misplaced logic, he would get nowhere. Cupcake believed he had found Frank Chater and was not, under any circumstances, for being shifted.

As far as he was concerned — protest all you wanted, spit out the anger at will — the man riding along of him, who had gunned the bushwhackers and settled the issue of the unsavoury characters who had just crossed their trail, was Frank Chater. If the fellow chose to ride under the name of John McCallam, so be it. A man was free to state his own name, any name he chose, in Cupcake's book.

But McCallam still had other ideas.

He was in no doubt now that he had only one way out of the fix. He would have to abandon the old man just short of North Bend. No choice. No room for second thinking. Just leave the fellow to make his own way into town, and then ride. Damn it, his whole future depended on it. He had to be free again. He had to be riding north — alone.

Soft, slow flurries of snow settled without a sound.

6

Cupcake's reckoning of a two-day ride to reach the outskirts of North Bend proved right to within an hour of full light on the third day.

'North Bend comin' up,' he announced, breaking a long silence between the two men. He reined his mount to a halt, eased the rope on the trailed horses and pointed ahead due north to the blurred shapes of the township. 'Less than an hour away.' He smiled with the obvious satisfaction of someone within reach of home. 'Sight for these old sore eyes and no mistake.'

He smacked his lips. 'I'd figure for Moses Fletcher to be openin' up the saloon time we ride in. Just right for him to rustle up one of them prairie-high breakfasts of his. Fella starts his day with one of Moses' breakfasts, and he's set for darn near a week. That prospect take your fancy, Mr Chater?'

McCallam sat his horse without a movement, his gaze sharp and steady on the outline of the town buildings, starkly black on the covering of deep snow, silent and seemingly lifeless at this hour. 'You need a doctor,' he murmured, holding the steady gaze. 'Breakfast can wait.'

'Suit yourself,' said Cupcake, with a resigned shrug of his shoulders. 'Don't make a deal of odds either way, come to think of it. Damnit, we've come this far; what's an hour or so to one of Moses' breakfasts? T'ain't worth a spit. Even so, a stiff measure would sure as hell put some life in these sore bones, eh? Ain't goin' to deny me that, are you?'

McCallam half-turned in the saddle. 'T'ain't goin' to be up to me, old man,' he said quietly. 'I shan't be there.'

Cupcake stayed silent for a moment, his tired eyes fixed on McCallam's face, his hands soft on the reins. 'You're tellin' me you ain't goin' on, that it?' he croaked at last, his voice thick and heavy, his breath shredding like a torn sheet from his mouth. 'You're pullin' out?'

'I'm sayin' just that. Like I've said, I ain't Frank Chater, but I'm sure as hell a prisoner on the run, and sooner or later there's goin' to be someone — just like Slater back there — who's tappin' me on the shoulder, or mebbe standin' to a shoot-out, or simply intent on draggin' me back to that hell-hole at Williamsville for somethin' I didn't do. Well, that ain't goin' to happen. I'm headin' north. Fast and free. Time ain't on my side, but what I've got I'll make the most of — and it don't include ridin' into North Bend to settle some dispute between a town and a man I've never met who'll probably shoot me in the back first chance he gets. T'ain't my business, old man. It's yours. It's the town's — but it ain't mine.'

Cupcake sat silent again, his gaze still steady, almost unblinking. He spat carefully, deliberately into the snow and shifted at his mount's unease. 'Ain't a deal I can do about that, is there, Mr Chater? I see your mind's settled, though I still ain't sure of the tale you've been spoutin' about the pen and all that. Still, no matter. You figured you'd see me this far, eh? Close enough, but not quite there.'

'I've told you before, I ain't no gunman! When are you goin' to get it into your head — ?'

'Yeah, yeah, I hear you, Mr Chater,' said Cupcake, gathering the reins in one hand as he tightened the trailed rope to the pommel. 'Well, now, you just carry right on there. Do just like you say, whatever your reasons. Me — well, I'll just ride on like you say and have Doc Tucker fix this leg here and while he's doin' it I'll explain to the others gathered round that, sure, I found Frank Chater — leastways he found me — and, sure, I saw what the fella could do: that he could shoot his way out of hell if need be. But no, he can't do it for us. Or mebbe won't do it for us. Could be he's got more pressin' matters to attend to. Bigger deals. Hell, when you come to reckon it, who are we, little old North Bend? About as noticeable as a stone in a creek bed. No, we won't be seein' Frank Chater, not now, not ever. We're just goin' to have to struggle on somehow till Royce Chisholm finally burns himself out, or there ain't nobody left for him to abuse and then shoot.'

Cupcake took a deep breath.

'But don't you fret none, Mr Chater,' he continued, making no attempt to hide the cutting cynicism in his voice. 'I'll think of somethin' to say to soothe them disappointed townsfolk. You bet I will. And you know somethin', they'll understand. Sure they will, 'cus they're like that. Decent-livin', God-fearin' folk who don't wish ill on a soul.'

Cupcake aimed a line of spittle across the snow, eased the wounded leg into a more comfortable position and urged his mount a few steps forward.

'Won't be for holdin' you up none,

Mr Chater. Guess you've got some distance to trail yet. Just remains for me to thank you again for savin' my life back there. I'd have been long stiff by now if you hadn't turned up when you did. Thanks. Anythin' here you want — blankets, food, ammunition — help yourself. Least I can do.'

The old man smiled, waited a moment, then ordered his mount on.

'Best keep movin', Mr Chater,' he called, without looking back. 'Weather's closin' in again.'

McCallam sat the mare in silence, his gaze flat and steady on the old man, the line of trailed horses, the scuffed snow, Cupcake's swirling breath and, in the far distance, the brooding shapes of the township where now the first fingers of smoke were twisting into the mass of grey sky.

Damn, he thought, on an angry grunt. Damn the trail he had ridden out of Williamsville, the snowline he had reached, the cabin, the body, the dead man's clothes.

And damn too his meeting up with Cupcake. Another half-mile in any other direction and he would have missed him; missed too hearing the story of North Bend.

And finally damn the fact that he was sitting his horse here in the snow-gripped wastelands outside North Bend, with the heavy skies threatening yet more falls, the cold biting deep into his bones and the wind whipping itself into what would soon strengthen to a blizzard.

He should be heading north beyond the town, putting still more distance between himself and whoever eventually trailed out of Williamsville when Slater's posse failed to return and their bodies were found in the snow.

It was only ever going to be a matter of time.

Well, he pondered, how much time did he have? How much did he need? Days, weeks, maybe as long as months? How far would that amount of time take him, and where would it lead? Or was there another way?

He grunted, shrugged himself deep into the buckskin jacket and reined the mare on to follow in the old man's tracks.

7

He looked a gunman. He had that same easy stance, the same seemingly loose but highly charged body and limbs. It was all there in the face, the gaunt but alert expression, the watchful eyes that followed wherever you moved and missed nothing. He was tall, dark-skinned, weathered; a man who had seen many things, experienced the best and worst that life could deliver and now maybe found nothing new in either other men or their lives. Oh, yes, he was a gunman.

And yet there was something — something that ran deep within the fellow — that seemed out of place.

Sheriff Jess Hart dismissed his thoughts, came to his feet behind his cleared desk in the office at North Bend, grunted softly to himself and poured a fresh mug of coffee from the steaming pot.

'I got a problem here, mister,' he began, letting his gaze move slowly from the concentrated faces of Henry Begine and Moses Fletcher to the expressionless stare of McCallam. 'I'm a man of the law; I wear the badge here and hold the position of sheriff. And that kinda puts me at odds with condonin' the hirin' of a gunman to settle a town problem, even though the deal has been privately arranged. You follow me? By all that's written in my own code of conduct, I should either arrest you, Frank Chater, as a wanted man and clap you tight behind bars until higher territorial authority decides what the hell to do with you. Or, if I happened to be feelin' generous, simply run you out of town with a warnin' not to show your face here again.'

'But that would be ridiculous,' blustered Henry Begine, fumbling his timepiece nervously across his ample paunch. 'A waste when we've finally got the chance — '

'Or,' said the sheriff, raising the mug

to silence Begine, 'I could reckon it only decent to offer my personal thanks for lookin' after old Cupcake in the way you did, savin' his life and bringin' him safely back to North Bend, and leave you to ride out in your own good time.'

'But before he rides,' interrupted Moses Fletcher, 'mebbe there'd be time — '

'Then there's a third alternative,' continued Hart. 'If I believe your story about bein' this fella John McCallam, an escaped prisoner out of Williamsville who's already stolen a horse and shot at least two guards, then I have no choice but to hand you back to the prison authorities. That'd be my duty.'

'Well, I for one do not believe such a story,' blustered Begine again, 'but I see the value of Mr Chater here stickin' to it. It's the obvious way, as Cupcake has said, to keep his true identity from Chisholm. What could be better? Chisholm won't ever have heard of John McCallam, but he just might have heard the name Frank Chater.'

'I agree,' said Moses Fletcher, nodding vigorously. 'The cover is perfect and I commend Mr Chater on figurin' it out. Very thorough. Very smart. But I guess deception's in the nature of your business, eh, Mr Chater?'

McCallam eased himself from the shadows into the soft glow of the lantern on the sheriff's desk. 'I've told you who I am. There's nothin' more to add.'

''Ceptin' you haven't told me why you rode into North Bend,' said Hart, tightening his gaze on McCallam. 'If you're who you say you are, you should've ridden on, stayed clear of towns, the law, anywhere you might be seen or recognized. You had no need to ride into North Bend. Cupcake would've made it well enough. Soon as Doc Tucker's through with him he'll confirm that, I'm sure. So what brings you here, mister?'

'The deal, o' course,' snapped Begine, slapping his paunch. 'The arrangement I have agreed between Mr Chater and the senior town men — Moses here,

Doc Tucker, Portly Mann and Ed Birch at the livery. Everyone of us decent, upstandin' fellas, as you well know. We have only the wellbein' of the town at heart. We must be rid of this man Chisholm before his evil buries us and leaves North Bend a ghost town.'

'Hear, hear,' echoed Moses. 'Whatever it takes. Whatever the cost.'

Sheriff Hart placed the coffee mug on his desk. 'And you, Mr Chater — or McCallam — what do you say? How deep into this deal are you, and how do you propose goin' about your part in the agreement? Only fair I should know, don't you reckon? After all, like I've said, I am the law here.'

Begine consulted his timepiece. 'And grateful you'll be, too, to have another gun — a professional gun — on our side,' he said, flourishing the piece back to his waistcoat pocket.

Hart shot the man a sharp, resentful glance. 'I ain't denyin' that, but Mr Chater here — if that's who he is

— remains a hired gun, and that is a situation — '

'Hold it,' said Moses anxiously, stepping closer to the office window. 'We've got company headin' this way. One of Chisholm's sidekicks. Scumbag by the name of Spreads Shard. Brute of a fella. All fists and mouth. You heard of him, Mr Chater?'

★ ★ ★

The man stamped snow from his boots on the boardwalk fronting Sheriff Hart's office, spat into the sludgy pools at his feet and crashed through the door banging it shut behind him.

Shard's sheer bulk and height seemed to fill the room and dim the glow of the lantern, so that the mere presence of the man threatened in the vastness of his shadow. He stood, legs apart, hands on hips, a last trim of snow melting softly on the brim of his broad hat, and stared like an irate crow at the sheriff. His eyes were narrowed to slits, his thin lips twisted

62

in the depth of the dirt and stubble darkening his face.

'That gripin' sonofabitch Cupcake rode in early this mornin' trailin' a line of horses. Stranger ridin' along of him. Right? So Mr Chishom wants to know how come and who the new face in town belongs to. And he wants to know now.'

Shard's voice was not so much a sound as a boom, hitting the four walls of the office like a wind building for a tornado, the words crashing from floor to ceiling, wall to wall as if in a frenzy to escape to the open street.

Sheriff Hart, forcing himself to appear relaxed and untroubled, replenished his coffee with a slow, deliberate, almost casual ease. 'I don't know,' he said at last from behind a misty screen of steam from the mug as he lifted it to his lips. 'Cupcake's business is his affair, not mine. Or Chisholm's. As I understand it, he's been attendin' to some out-of-town matters. You want to know more, you'd best ask him.' He

63

sipped slowly at the coffee. 'Seems like he got himself bushwhacked and badly wounded while he was out there. Stranger saved his life and brought him home. Cupcake's with Doc Tucker right now. That's as much as I know.'

Shard glared, craning his bullneck forward, his eyes still narrowed, fists clenched. Henry Begine fingered his timepiece nervously. Moses Fletcher settled his grip on the lapels of his jacket. McCallam remained in the shadows behind the low glow of the lantern.

'So who's the stranger?' grunted Shard.

'Ask him yourself,' said Hart. 'He's right here.'

Shard's glare tightened as his head turned slowly, left to right, the narrowed eyes taking in the faces he knew, then settling again on Hart. 'Where?' he growled.

'Right here.'

McCallam stepped forward just far enough for his face to move out of shadow into the soft yellow glow. 'What's your problem, fella?'

Shard's lips broke through the stubble in a cracked grin that revealed stained, chipped teeth. 'No problem — leastways not for me. You just get yourself to see Mr Chisholm right now. He's waitin' for you at the saloon.'

McCallam's expression remained unmoved, his stare gathering like a build up of darkness to prelude bad weather. 'Mebbe I will, mebbe I won't,' he said quietly. 'I ain't in no hurry. I've got other business to look to.'

'No mebbe about it, mister.' Shard's grin twisted to a scowl. 'Right now means just that. Now!'

Begine's fingers skidded like flies over his timepiece. Fletcher lost his grip on his lapels. Sheriff Hart replaced the mug on his desk without shifting his gaze from McCallam's face. He had seen the watchful look begin to deepen.

'I said mebbe, and in my time.'

The tone of McCallam's voice was even, steady, but definite. Not a word was lost or misunderstood.

Shard's clenched fists eased before tightening again like rocks. 'I don't like your tone, mister. I don't like it one bit.'

'Shame,' said McCallam, moving to the office door. He grinned. 'You've got my answer. Now go deliver it.'

He opened the door with a flourish that filled the office with a blast of icy air.

Shard hesitated. He glanced quickly at Sheriff Hart, at Begine and Fletcher, then, without warning and surprisingly fast for his size launched himself at McCallam.

The sheer bulk and weight of the sidekick propelled McCallam through the open door to the boardwalk, where he slipped on the icy surface, lost his balance and was forced to grab the nearest support. He held on to the veranda post, gathering his breath, struggling for a foothold and could only watch as Shard's bulk bore down on him like a rumbling storm cloud.

He swayed to the left, at the same

time cleaving the side of his hand across Shard's throat with a shuddering force. The man spluttered, choked, fell forward and staggered, clutching at his neck, into the street where he collapsed face-down in the snow.

When he stirred, found his breath and the croaking remnants of his voice, he came clumsily to his knees, then his feet, groaned a deep curse and stumbled away through a flurry of snowflakes.

'Now tell me that ain't Frank Chater,' murmured Begine to Sheriff Hart's ear at the open doorway.

8

North Bend's day began on a more optimistic note than it had for many weeks. Cupcake was back in town; true, he had taken lead at the hands of bushwhackers, but a fellow name of McCallam had saved his life, brought him safely home and, a whole sight more to the point, had whipped Chisholm's sonofabitch sidekick, Spreads Shard, and taught him a lesson he had not known, or felt, in years, if not in his lifetime. Yessir, somebody — this unknown fellow, a complete stranger — had done what no man forty miles in any direction would ever have reckoned possible let alone dared to do.

And the news of it spread and gathered depth faster than the snowfall.

'I hear tell as how the ground shook when Shard hit the street.'

'And flat on his face at that.'

'They're sayin' as how that fella McCallam's hands are set like rock. They reckon he could crack a skull.'

'With one hand!'

'Shard ain't goin' to like this one bit.'

'He'll hit back like a tornado.'

'Chisholm along of him, not to mention that other snake, Deloit. Hell, they could take this town apart.'

'And most of us with it.'

'So who is this fella McCallam? Where's he hail from? What's he do?'

'Who cares? I ain't fussed. Any man who can whip Shard and stand his ground gets my backin'. And no questions asked.'

'Let's hope the fella hangs around a while . . .'

But that was already the trouble for McCallam. He had no intention of remaining in North Bend a day longer than necessary. He had done right by Cupcake, seen him into Doc Tucker's hands and told Sheriff Hart as much of the story as he needed to know. Cupcake would tell his own version of events in time.

Meanwhile, McCallam had insisted to the sheriff and the other town elders that he was who he said he was: John McCallam. He was not Frank Chater, the professional gunman they had hired and had expected to ride into North Bend. Not, he knew, that they had for one moment believed him, or ever would. They were content in their belief that McCallam was a cover name to hide his true identity from Royce Chisholm. And that was how things were going to remain no matter what he said or did.

The episode with Shard had been a mistake. Maybe he should have let the sidekick have his way; maybe he should have gone to face Chisholm, said as little as possible and done nothing. That way he might have been free to leave North Bend whenever he chose.

Now he was not so sure of his freedom. Could North Bend become another prison? Had he swapped the pen at Williamsville for the iron bars of a remote North Dakota town?

Sheriff Hart was already confirming McCallam's worst fear.

'I know Chisholm. I know the way he reacts, the way his crazed thinkin' takes him. I know because I've had the rat under my skin for long enough. And that's why, Mr McCallam, or Chater, or whoever you are, I'm goin' along with Begine and the others in spite of bein' a lawman. What they plan and appear to have arranged is against the law in every way. But, and it's a big but, there don't seem to be a second choice here — leastways not without a whole barrel of blood bein' spilled. It ain't worth seein' decent townfolk die. I need help, another gun at my side — and I ain't fussed one bit if it ain't legal. No price is too high to be rid of Chisholm and the scum standin' to him. You'll know that well enough, Mr McCallam, when you meet him — which you will. And soon . . . '

The calm almost comforting warmth of Hart's office might have seemed like a haven for a man in McCallam's position, but he knew such an impression was as false as the prospect of a heatwave.

Hart had watched his face intently throughout his explanation of his own dilemma as if exploring it, or perhaps waiting for the tell-tale shift of some mask.

'So, what you plannin', mister?' he asked, pouring fresh mugs of hot coffee to which he added generous measures of whiskey.

'Do I have choices?'

Hart shrugged. 'Depends who you are, don't it? What would Frank Chater do? Well, by my figurin', he'd sit it out, wait for Chisholm to come to him. That's a top gunman's way. He waits. He watches. He listens. And he don't talk too much. Professionals don't talk. Talkin' breaks the concentration. Or so I'm told. Is that your experience, Mr McCallam?'

'Mebbe.'

Hart grunted. 'O' course, I ain't too

sure what McCallam would do. I don't know him. Is he a gunman, a professional, a sonofabitch with no morals, no scruples, no feelin's even, who shoots to kill on the price of the purse? Or is he somebody else? I wouldn't know. Would you?'

This time McCallam shrugged. 'Mebbe,' he repeated.

'There is another way,' added Hart hurriedly. 'Either one of these fellas could ride out. Right now. Turn his back on North Bend and its troubles and simply disappear. It's unlikely Chisholm would follow with the weather set like it is. Shard would nurse a sore head for a few days, but he'd get over it. 'Course, then the real vengeance would begin. Chisholm would be lookin' for payback. And he'd take it, any way he chose; anybody, anywhere, anytime.' Hart crossed to the window, cupping his hands round the warm mug. 'Would Chater ride? Is he that sort of fella? Does he turn his back? Has he ever, on anythin'? Gunmen never show their backs to nobody, do they? That's what I'm told. I ain't never seen it for fact.'

He turned to face McCallam. 'And what about McCallam?' he said, raising his eyebrows. 'What would he do? I know what I'd do if I was him: I'd ride. No messin'. I'd be out of here fast as my horse would carry me. And I wouldn't look back. Just go, and keep goin'. You bet. After all, North Bend and Chisholm ain't McCallam's problems, are they? Nothin' to do with him. Or would he have conscience? Would he consider it only decent to help out, lend a hand where he could? He might. He might be just that sort; a carin', thinkin', feelin' man. They do exist. They ain't all like Chisholm. But, like I say, I don't know.'

Hart replaced his mug on the desk and crossed to the far wall where his heavy coat hung forlornly on its peg. 'Time I did my rounds. Folk'll be wantin' to know how Cupcake's gettin' on.' He slipped into the coat, adjusted the set across his broad shoulders, and buttoned it high into the neck. 'They'll also be askin' about you, mister. So what'll I tell them, eh?'

★ ★ ★

Sheriff Hart was still some distance from Doc Tucker's home at the far end of the town's main street when two youths hailed him and trudged excitedly through the snow to join him on the boardwalk.

'Mornin', Sheriff,' said the leaner of the two, touching the brim of his hat respectfully. 'Me and my friend Bart here were kinda wonderin' if it's true — that is to say, if it's a fact what we're hearin'. We guessed you of all folk would know.'

Hart eyed the two fellows patiently. 'Know what?' he asked.

'About the gunman,' whispered the second youth, looking round him anxiously. 'The one in town. Rode in with Cupcake. We hear as how he's given that sidekick Shard a whippin'.'

'So who is he, Mr Hart?' hissed the leaner youth. 'He one of them hired fellas from back East? Does he wear a fancy waistcoat?'

'All them hired guns wear fancy waistcoats,' added his friend.

The two youths nodded in unison.

'Well now,' began the sheriff, 'I don't know anythin' about a hired gun in town, fancy waistcoated or otherwise. All I know is that a gent by the name of McCallam kindly lent a helpin' hand to Cupcake when the old fella ran into a spot of bother, and saw him safely home.'

'He the one who whipped Spreads Shard?'

'Mr McCallam did have somethin' of an altercation with Shard earlier on in which he stood his ground and made his point with some force, but that ain't no reason for you young fellas to go spreadin' rumours about gunmen from back East wearin' fancy waistcoats. Mr McCallam is a perfectly ordinary sort of fella.' Sheriff Hart grunted and stood to his full height. 'Why, I'd wager fella like him ain't never owned a fancy waistcoat let alone worn one.'

The two youths exchanged hurried glances

'T'ain't what we're hearin', Mr Hart,' said the leaner youth.

'Oh, and just who's dreamin' up these stories you're hearin'?'

'Everybody. It's all over town, Mr Hart. All over.'

'He's right. They say the fella's here to gun Royce Chisholm. Is that a fact?'

Hart grunted again. 'It is not. There is no hired gun in town. Like I say, McCallam is just — '

'Mebbe he's the gunman,' said the lean youth's partner. He blinked as his eyes widened. 'Yeah ... mebbe it's McCallam. Could be him, couldn't it, Mr Hart? What do you reckon?'

'As far as I'm concerned — '

Sheriff Hart's words were lost in the sudden eruption across the tight morning air of a riot of shouts, a woman's screams, a gunshot, the crash of splintering furniture, heavy boots crunching across broken glass, the high-pitched creaking protest of the Saddles saloon's batwings as Spreads Shard burst through them on to the board-walk like a lathered bull in a snorting rage.

His eyes bulged, his chest lifted and fell through the struggled effort of breathing. He glared round him. 'Where is he? Where's the sonofabitch?'

A group of town men had gathered in a huddled group on the opposite side of the street.

'You lookin' for McCallam?' called one of the men.

'That's him,' snarled Shard. 'That's the one.'

'Try the livery.'

Shard spat, winced at the pain in his neck, then stomped through calf-deep snow towards the livery, a Colt gleaming like silver in his grubby hand.

9

'Idiots!' Sheriff Hart glowered at the huddled group of town men as he trudged through the snow in pursuit of Shard, the two youths frisking like puppies in his wake. 'What the hell's goin' on here?'

'Shard's been rilin' himself up in the saloon there ever since McCallam gave him that whippin',' said one of the men pulling his coat collar high into his neck. 'Boozed through by now, I'd reckon.'

'McCallam in the livery?' asked Hart.

'Saw him headin' that way soon after you left your office.'

A pale-faced, wet-eyed man rubbed his hands together for warmth. 'Mebbe he'll finish Shard this time. Gun him for the rat he is.'

Hart grunted and trudged on, his breath swirling round him in a misty shawl. 'Stay clear, you hear. And one of you go fetch Doc Tucker. I've got a feelin' we're goin' to need him.'

Shard had reached the livery yard where the forge steamed and glowed like some fat black beast, melting the snow around it, when Hart fired a warning shot high above the hench-man's head.

'Hold it right there, Shard,' he called, taking a deep breath against the effort of battling the snowfall. 'There ain't no need for this. Put that gun down and let's all get ourselves back in the warm. You hearin' me there?'

Shard hesitated, turned, one hand clamped to his neck. His face gleamed with pulsing veins and a sweat that clung like frost to his stubble. His stare seemed frozen as if seeing into a white empty space. He spat and blazed his Colt wildly in Hart's direction, then turned again and plunged across the yard to the stabling.

'Damn the man!' cursed Hart, heaving his already aching legs into motion again, at the same time catching a glimpse of livery proprietor Ed Birch lurking fearfully at the side of the stables. 'Just keep out of it, Ed,' he muttered to himself. 'Don't do nothin' stupid. Don't even think . . . '

But too late. Shard stumbled to a halt, steadied the Colt and let it roar through a single shot to send Ed Birch spinning across the snow to a crumpled, twitching heap clutching at a free-bleeding wound to his shoulder.

'Hell!' cursed Hart again, reaching the melted snow of the yard, his face tingling with the sudden rush of heat from the forge.

Shard had wrenched open one of the stable's double doors and stood now on the threshold, peering into the gloom.

'That's far enough, Shard,' called Hart, from the far side of the yard. 'Leave it right there. Let's just — '

Shard swung round, the Colt blazing a spray of loose fire, before launching himself into the depths of the stables.

Horses snorted, whinnied, stamped.

Ed Birch groaned as he rolled through the bloodstained snow. The forge released a cloud of smoke and hissed what might have been its anger.

'Doc's on his way, Mr Hart,' wheezed the leaner youth, scrambling into the yard.

'What the hell you doin' here?' croaked Hart, only half aware of the youth as he watched the stable doors.

'Me and Bart here wanna see how McCallam handles a gun,' grinned the youth. 'We ain't never seen a full-fledged gunman at work.'

'He ain't no gunman and this ain't the time . . . ' began Hart, but let the words drift away as the door swung open and McCallam stepped from the gloom leading Spreads Shard behind him on a length of rope securing the side-kick's hands.

'What the . . . ?' hissed the sheriff, his brow creasing to a deep frown.

The youths stared open-mouthed, eyes as round as frozen moons. 'See that . . . ' murmured one, as McCallam led Shard to the livery yard's fencing and tied him to it.

'He's all yours, Sheriff,' called McCallam.

The morning darkened as a light snow began to fall.

* * *

'Gave him another whippin' and then made him look a complete fool,' grinned a thin man wrapped in coats and scarves as he warmed his hands at the stove in Henry Begine's crowded store. 'Should've seen him! I ain't had a better laugh in weeks! Took the scumbag a whole twenty minutes to persuade Sheriff Hart to untie him. Chisholm would've run riot if he hadn't.'

'So where's Shard now?' asked Portly Mann, the town barber.

'Back in the saloon, nursin' his pride as well as his bruises — and keepin' well clear of Chisholm who ain't none too pleased with him.'

An old-timer blew a cloud of smoke through the charred bowl of his cherrywood pipe. 'T'ain't Shard who'll get to sufferin', is it? We all know where Chisholm will seek his retribution — and that'll be on us.'

'Mebbe McCallam will get to him first; call him to a showdown right there in the street where we can all witness it.'

'Ain't nobody seen the fella draw a piece yet, let alone fire it,' piped a younger man from behind a pile of blankets.

The men and women gathered in the store's warm, comfortable atmosphere murmured among themselves. A small boy pressed his nose to the candy jar. A young girl fingered a display of ribbons. The youths, who had followed Sheriff Hart to the livery, lounged at the side of the flour bins, their eyes darting like birds to the street, watchful as ever for a sight of McCallam.

Henry Begine fussed and dusted behind his counter wishing he had a dollar for every person seeking shelter, comfort and maybe solace in the store's four walls. The small boy's hand darted to a box of biscuits and snaffled one into his pocket. He blushed when the old-timer winked at him.

'How's Ed Birch? Anybody hear?' asked one of the women, hugging a wicker basket to her.

'Sheriff helped Doc Tucker carry him to Doc's place,' said a man with a patch over one eye. 'Swapping stories with Cupcake right now, I'll wager.'

'Damn lucky he didn't get himself killed,' said Portly. 'Shard was in a flamin' mood. Worst I've seen him.'

'And I'm for reckonin' that's only the start of it,' piped the old-timer from behind another cloud of pipe smoke.

'So who is this fella McCallam?' frowned a thick-shouldered man, plunging his hands into the pockets of his fur-collared coat. 'What do we know for certain, apart from the fact he saved Cupcake's life and brought him home? Is he a gunman, a professional from somewhere back East? Is he hired? If so, who hired him? What was he doin' at the livery? Was he gettin' ready to pull out? Wouldn't have got far in this snow. Like it or not he's got to stay in town. No choice, not till the weather lifts and a thaw sets in. And while ever he's here he's goin' to have Chisholm scratchin' at his back, if not shootin' him first chance he gets.'

The gathering murmured again. The old-timer repacked his pipe. Portly Mann lifted his derby and smoothed his oiled hair. The small boy stuffed the snaffled biscuit into his mouth. The young girl turned her attention to a display of bonnets. The two youths watched the empty, snowbound street and the still thickening winter clouds.

Henry Begine tried not to catch anyone's eye as he polished the counter for the twentieth time and shifted the candy jar clear of the boy's nose.

'What do you reckon, Henry?' said the old-timer. 'You've met this fella McCallam. What sort of a man is he?'

Begine stopped polishing, left the

duster where it lay and stood back from the counter. 'I'd figure for him bein' a very resourceful man. You wouldn't fool him none. And you wouldn't mess with him neither, as Spreads Shard found out.'

'But is he a gunman — and a hired gun at that?' persisted the man in the fur-collared coat. 'That's what we're askin'.'

Begine hesitated, studying the faces of the townfolk. 'I'd say he's a gunman. Yes, I'd reckon that — not that I have a deal of experience on these matters you understand. Sheriff Hart knows far more about such men than myself.' He smiled weakly, felt a beading of sweat on his brow and rested a hand on the duster.

A lean man with a slouched stance slid his arm round a young woman's waist. 'I heard talk as how you and Moses Fletcher hired the fella. That a fact, Mr Begine?'

'I heard the same,' echoed the man with a patch over one eye. 'And I heard as how Cupcake and Sheriff Hart are in on the deal.'

Begine's fingers clawed deep into the duster. 'Well,' he began, conscious of the sweat thickening, 'I suppose there is — '

'Here he comes!' announced the leaner of the two youths watching the street. 'McCallam. Leaving the sheriff's office and headin' . . . Hell, looks like he's set on visitin' the saloon!'

10

The town's eyes settled on McCallam. They stared from windows, dark doorways, shadowy alleys where the snowfall was thinner, some gathered in close groups, pressed shoulder-to-shoulder for warmth. An old man huddled in coats, scarves and sacking shawls, followed the man's steps from the boardwalk fronting Portly Mann's barbering shop. His equally aged dog waited at his side, his sad eyes unaware of the sudden interest and excitement.

Those gathered in Henry Begine's store had pressed themselves as close to the windows as possible, their heads bobbing and craning for a better view as the man walked on down the street, his feet seeming to fall instinctively where there was an already trodden path, wagon wheel ruts, and the footsteps of others to follow. He walked in silence, steadily, easily; no hurry, no anxiety, almost as if out for a stroll. And his gaze ahead never shifted.

The two youths kept up a running commentary, murmured first to themselves from their icy vantage point outside the store, and then relayed to those inside.

'He ain't slipped once.'

'It's like he knows every darned inch of the street dirt he can't see.'

'That's a gunman if you like. All gunman walk like that, specially when they're on a mission. I read all about it in one of them Eastern magazines.'

'He's all pieced up, I reckon. Them twin Colts 'neath that buckskin jacket?'

'Sure to be. That's what gunmen wear, ain't it?'

'I don't know. I ain't never seen a real live gunman — and definitely not in this town!'

'Look at his eyes . . . '

It was the woman with the wicker basket who interrupted the flow of words.

'Mebbe we should go call Sheriff Hart,' she suggested to Begine.

'Why should we?' frowned the storekeeper. 'Fella ain't doin' any harm, is he? All he's doin' is walkin' down the street. Since when has that been a crime around here?'

'He's headin' for the saloon,' said the man with the patch over one eye.

'So? That ain't unlawful neither.'

The old-timer relit his pipe. 'Mebbe he fancies a drink,' he puffed.

'Yeah, mebbe he does at that,' agreed Begine, nodding his head.

The small boy snaffled another biscuit watched by the girl fingering the ribbons. He stuck his tongue out at her when she frowned a look of admonishment.

'Come to think of it, I could use a drink myself,' added Begine, swishing the duster through a final polish of the counter. 'Anyone care to join me?'

'Count me in,' grinned the old-timer.

'Me too,' said the man in the fur-collared coat.

'Right, that's it then,' beamed Begine. 'Store's closed, folks till after lunch.'

'McCallam's nearly there,' called the leaner youth from the boardwalk. 'Who do you reckon's waitin' on him?'

*　　*　　*

Small groups and lines of townfolk, including those from the store, shadowed McCallam in silence, his every step, every movement, pause, hesitation as he found a footing, mirrored in their own. When he reached the three steps to the saloon, stamped the snow from his boots as he mounted them, and halted within a few feet of the batwings, they seemed to hold their breath, tensed in the seconds of waiting for the man's next move.

McCallam adjusted his collar, ran a finger over the brim of his hat and laid a hand on the 'wings. The creak of their old hinges might have been heard for miles around, such was the stillness and silence in the street.

The old-timer narrowed his eyes through a cloud of pipe smoke; the women shoppers gripped their shopping baskets. Breath swirled like blown mist. The two youths had dared to cross the street and position themselves at the side of the saloon, all set to pounce for a front-row view once McCallam passed through the 'wings. They did not have long to wait.

'Follow me,' said Henry Begine, gesturing to the old-timer and the man in the fur-collared coat.

Portly Mann and two other townmen summoned the courage to join them. A dozen men crowded the boardwalk. The women stood apart, huddled in murmured conversation, glancing anxiously from time to time at the unmoving 'wings and the shadowy depths beyond them.

'Has anybody warned the sheriff of what's happenin' here?' asked one of the women with a haughty flick of a hand at a straying feather in her bonnet. 'Somebody should, you know. Definitely.'

'I'll go,' said the young girl, pulling herself free of the man with the slouched stance.

'And tell him to hurry,' added a woman in a long black skirt and a clutter of shawls across her shoulders.

The young girl lifted her skirts above her ankles and made her way back down the street, the man slipping and sliding behind her.

'Now we'll see,' said the woman, flicking again at the straying feather. 'This is goin' to be work for the law.'

The women huddled closer.

★ ★ ★

McCallam relished the sudden flush of warmth as he stood in the smoky gloom of the bar and waited for his eyes to adjust to the dimmer light.

There was no more than a scattering of townmen at the scrubbed tables. Two were into a game of cards, but paused in the deal as the 'wings creaked open. Three men sat at a corner table, a

94

half-empty bottle of whiskey resting between them, a pale-faced, tight-bosomed bar girl lounging half-heartedly close by. One man stood alone at the bar, his back to the 'wings. He turned at the sound of McCallam's steps, nodded, mouthed an inaudible greeting, finished his drink in a single gulp and eased away into the deeper shadows.

McCallam moved to the bar where a tall, beanpole of a fellow with a bald head, a beaky nose and long, bony fingers fanned out like weeds on the bar, waited to serve him. 'What's your preference, mister?' he asked, through a well-used smile.

'Lookin' for a room,' said McCallam, conscious of the customers' eyes fixed on him. 'Two, three days — leastways till the weather eases some and I can push on north.'

The barman's smile faded. A thin beading of sweat broke down the sides of his beaky nose. He glanced quickly behind him. 'Well, I ain't sure . . . ' he began, but let the words ebb away as

Moses Fletcher appeared at the far end of the bar like a shape slid into place.

'Mr McCallam,' beamed the proprietor. He gestured openly with a glowing cigar clamped between manicured fingers. 'You're right about the weather out there. Certainly ain't no conditions for travellin'. I hear say as how there's drifts close on a man's height to the north. And as for the trail headin' that way, well, I for one wouldn't — '

'No rooms for hire,' boomed a voice from the stairs that led to the shadowed first floor. 'Not now, not in the future. And specially not to you, mister.'

The last words had dripped from Royce Chisholm's mouth like a venom that sizzled even as they hit the air.

The man trod heavily, deliberately down the stairs, halted halfway and glared at McCallam with a look of simmering contempt. He was a large man, thick-boned, bulky, his skin taut and tanned as if he had ridden for weeks head-on into a wild wind. The eyes were set deep, yet flickered like flames. Some in town reckoned Chisholm could see out of the back of his head. McCallam could believe it.

Lurking only two steps behind him was the man forever referred to as Chisholm's shadow. Deloit, as he chose to be known, was lean, lithe, sharp as a rattler and twice as lethal. He killed — blade, bullet or any other means suited him equally well — without a second thought or the slightest regret. He was, in fact, the complete professional killer and, dressed as ever in his familiar dark shirt, pants, boots and tooled leather waistcoat, looked every stitch and button the part.

Two steps behind him, was the bulk of Spreads Shard, or what to McCallam's reckoning looked to be a sadly crumpled but still seething version of the sidekick. He had a permanent snarl scrawled across his swollen lips.

'I figure you know who I am, mister,' said Chisholm. 'I certainly know who you are, so we'll cut the introductions and get to the point of my offer to you.

It comes just this once. Accept it or I shoot you right here, right now.' He grinned cynically. 'You hearin' me clear, fella?'

'About that room,' said McCallam calmly, carefully.

'Well, it's like I said . . . ' spluttered Fletcher, but went no further as Chisholm took two more steps down the stairs and aimed a line of spittle accurately into the spittoon only feet from McCallam's boots.

'Hey, scumbag, I'm talkin' to you.' Chisholm's stare hardened, the flame in his eyes directed at no one save McCallam. 'When I talk to somebody — '

'It's McCallam to you. But right now I ain't got neither the time nor the inclination to pay you much heed. So if you'll excuse me I got business to attend to here.'

The beanpole barman swallowed. 'What'll it be?' he managed to croak.

'Whiskey. And you can leave the bottle. I ain't goin' no place.'

11

The bar girl fidgeted nervously with the neckline of her dress. The card players did not move. Moses Fletcher hardly noticed the ash that spilled from his cigar across his waistcoat. A man at McCallam's back tried desperately to swallow, but could only croak on a sand-dry throat.

Chisholm tapped a finger along the butt of his holstered Colt. 'Got a lip on you, I see,' he grinned. 'Big talk, mister. You that big a man?'

McCallam poured a measure of whiskey from the bottle, drank it, replaced the glass on the bar and poured another. He remained silent, his stare fixed rigidly ahead.

'Not so big, I figure,' said Chisholm, easing down the last of the stairs, Deloit shadowing his every step. 'Big talkers never are in my experience. I've heard most of 'em. Killed a few in passin'.' He relaxed his weight on one hip. 'All the same come the showdown. Just words.' He nodded to Deloit to move to the bar. Shard stayed close in the shadows. 'So, seein' as how it's talk you're interested in, I'll spell out my offer real slow. That way you ain't goin' to miss a thing, are you? Not one word.'

Deloit moved to McCallam's side, his eyes fixed hawk-like on his face as if mapping every line of it.

'There ain't no rooms here, are there, Fletcher?' said Chisholm.

'As a matter of fact — ' began the saloon owner.

'I'll say that again,' snapped Chisholm. 'There ain't no rooms. So you, mister, are goin' to have to move, like it or not. And by move, I mean out of town, back to the trail — if you can find one.' Chisholm's finger tapped across the gun butt again. 'That clear enough for you, fella? Plain speakin', plain words.'

McCallam sank the measure of

whiskey in silence.

'Course,' continued Chisholm, 'if you ain't for takin' up my offer, then I'm left with only one choice: I'm goin' to have to shoot you, which, when you come to reckon it, might be a whole sight more painless than dyin' out there in the snow and cold. You figure, mister?'

McCallam stayed silent. A new length of ash grew on Fletcher's cigar. The beaky-nosed barman ran a glass-cloth over the counter. One of the card players thought about coming to his feet, took one look at the menacing bulk of Shard and sat down again. The gathering at the batwings seemed unaware of the freezing air and the scattering falls of snow. Inside the bar, only yards from where McCallam was standing, Henry Begine, the old-timer, the man in the fur-collared coat, and Portly Mann, watched in silence and without a movement between the four of them. A trickle of cold sweat inched its way down the bar girl's neck.

McCallam reached for the bottle of whiskey only to have his hand clamped to the bar by Deloit's iron grip. The men stared at each other. Deloit smiled. Chisholm grinned.

'I figure you've mebbe had your last drink, Mr McCallam,' hissed the henchman. 'Time's all out for you, unless you're goin' to — '

McCallam's clamped hand shifted with the speed and suddenness of a riled rattler, reversing the situation instantly as his own hand broke free of Deloit's grip and dropped like a rock on the gunman's.

Deloit winced, cursed, screwed his eyes at the drilling pain as the pressure from McCallam's hand cracked his little finger, then took hold of his wrist and wrenched his arm to the middle of his back.

McCallam pushed Deloit forward into Chisholm's path, at the same time drawing and levelling his Colt on the advancing Shard and the unsteady bulks of Chisholm and Deloit.

The bar girl shuddered. The card players jumped to their feet, scattering the cards and sending the chairs crashing to the floor. The barman retrieved the half-empty bottle of whiskey. Moses Fletcher's cigar dusted an even thicker cloud of ash across his waistcoat. Henry Begine had taken a step forward when the batwings swung open and Sheriff Hart trod snow into the bar.

'All right,' he called, 'let's hold it right there.' He ranged the barrel of a Winchester round the bar. Snow slid from the folds of his long coat to form puddles of water at his feet. His gaze was deep, steady and unblinking. Moses Fletcher began to speak but lost his nerve as Chisholm pushed Deloit to one side and glared like a hawk deprived of its prey at the threat of the rifle barrel.

'Don't nobody shift so much as a finger,' said Hart. A splash of melted snow fell from the brim of his hat. 'So what's all this about?'

'McCallam here — ' began Moses.

'All the fella asked — ' clipped the barman.

'It's obvious no man can travel — ' snapped Begine.

'He weren't even — ' offered Portly Mann.

'One at a time, f'Chris'sake!' shouted Hart above the babble of voices and jumble of words. He steadied the rifle, his gaze flicking instinctively to Deloit, then to Shard.

Chisholm's glare eased. 'A timely arrival, Sheriff,' he smiled, tapping the bar for the beanpole barman to serve him. 'I'm delighted to see you've come round to my way of thinkin' and are keepin' a careful eye on any undesirable strangers in town. This man McCallam here ain't wanted. Get rid of him. Or shall I get one of the boys to do your job for you?'

'I'm still the law in North Bend,' seethed Hart. 'I'm wearin' the badge, and there'll be no — '

'This is all an unfortunate mistake,' soothed Henry Begine, taking another step forward, his tensed expression relaxing to his storekeeper's gentle smile. 'All Mr McCallam was askin' — quite rightly in my view, bearin' in mind the state of the trail out there — was simple enough: might he have a room for a few days until the weather eases? As it happens, our kindly host Moses, can't at this time, see his way clear to providin' a room.'

Begine spread his arms in a conciliatory gesture. 'Understandable enough. Supply and demand and all that. It happens in the best run business. But in this instance there is an answer.' His smile spread to a beam. 'I can provide a room. Oh, yes, I have spare accommodation above the store and offer it gladly — and in the interests of town goodwill — to Mr McCallam for as long as he deems it necessary to remain here.'

The storekeeper swished aside his coat and hooked his thumbs into the slit pockets of his waistcoat. 'Does that solve the problem, Sheriff?' he asked, flushed with the spreading beam.

There was a tense, uncomfortable silence as Sheriff Hart looked quickly from Begine to McCallam then directly into the fast returning glare in Chisholm's eyes. Deloit nursed an aching arm. Shard stiffened but stayed silent and did not move.

'Seems like a good arrangement to me,' said Moses, returning to his cigar to blow a cloud of smoke ahead of him. 'Damn decent of you to make the offer, Henry. Real neighbourly.'

'It's no problem at all,' smiled Begine.

Chisholm's patience broke. 'When you've all done bein' so sonofabitch friendly, I'll remind you one more time who's runnin' this town.' The glare flared and spread across the faces watching him. 'Me — I run this town. And I say who comes, who goes, when and how, and don't let nobody forget it.' He focused on McCallam. 'As for you, mister, I've taken a real dislike to you. Same goes for my boys. But, just to show what a generous and compassionate fella I am, you can have the room at the store — for just as long as I say. You understand? You're here at my biddin'. When I say go, you'll go.'

McCallam was at the point of speaking when Sheriff Hart laid a restraining hand on his arm. 'So let's just clear this bar, eh? Get back to somethin' like normal. Mr McCallam, Henry, if you'll follow me we'll go get this matter of the room settled, shall we? The rest of you fellas back off. Either take your drink quietly, or go home. All right, let's move.'

The card players collected the scattered cards and began a new game. The bar girl pulled up a chair and joined them, her gaze still flicking nervously to Deloit. Chisholm called for a bottle of whiskey and three glasses and eased away with his sidekicks to the deepest corner of the bar where he sat with his back to the wall.

The beak-nosed barman polished glasses; Fletcher wreathed himself in a cloud of cigar smoke and ash.

'Clear some space here,' ordered

Hart, pushing open the batwings on the still crowded boardwalk. 'There ain't nothin' to see. Time you got yourselves back in the warm. T'aint no sort of day for standin' about.'

The crowd murmured, lingered, but slowly began to disperse, the town ladies huddling for one last gossip before clutching their baskets to them and stepping out to the snow.

'Your place, Henry,' ordered Hart again, shepherding the storekeeper and McCallam ahead of him. 'We've got some serious talkin' to do.'

They had gone less than a dozen steps when Doc Tucker hailed them from the top of the street, his bag clutched firmly in one hand, a stick to keep his balance in the other.

'My services needed back there?' he called.

'No problems, Doc,' answered Hart. 'Get back to your patients.' Doc waved and turned away. 'Mebbe I should've added, not yet,' murmured the sheriff to himself.

12

McCallam backed away from the window of the room overlooking the street and watched as Deloit strolled casually through the batwings of the Saddles saloon opposite and gazed slowly from left to right.

The gunslinger lit a cheroot, blew smoke and drew the folds of his coat around him. Stray flakes of snow danced on the icy wind that blew from the north. The sky lay heavy and grey; the air bit with the crisp sharpness of deep winter. A deserted, draughty boardwalk fronting the saloon in an equally deserted street was no place to be of choice, thought McCallam, his eyes narrowed on Deloit. Not unless you were looking, or perhaps waiting for somebody.

He eased another half step back as the gunslinger's gaze lifted to explore the windows above the store. 'Lookin' for me,' he murmured to himself. 'Help yourself, fella. You've got a choice.'

There were three rooms above the store: one used as a storeroom, the second as a spare room, and the third occupied by Begine as his private quarters. All three at the moment were in darkness.

'Stayin' here will be safer than the saloon,' Begine had insisted. 'And you can, o' course, for as long as it takes.'

'Till the trail's open again,' McCallam had said. 'Then I'm gone. This is no place for me.'

Begine had simply smiled and winked knowingly. 'As you wish, Mr Chater — sorry, McCallam.'

Sheriff Hart had grunted and cleared his throat hurriedly. 'Judgin' by what I've seen so far this whole situation could get out of hand just like that,' he had said, clicking his fingers. 'You ain't exactly made a favourable impression on Chisholm and his sidekicks, have you?'

'Nobody orders me about, not no how, and 'specially not since — ' But McCallam had let the words drift away. 'Anyway, who is Chisholm? How come he's here? What's he want, f'Chris'sake, a whole town to himself?'

'Precisely that,' Begine had murmured, his expression shading to a sullen grey.

'Fella rode in one day and before you could blink he was runnin' the place, gettin' them scumbags of his to do most of the dirty work, and just, well — ' Hart had stumbled.

'And we allowed it to happen. We didn't stir till it was all too late,' Begine had added. 'That's when we — mainly myself — sent for you. The rest you know.'

But that was the point, pondered McCallam, still watching the saloon, he did not know and would never have known anything of this had he not escaped from the pen, found the forest cabin and assumed the identity of a dead man. Slipping into that buckskin jacket had been a big mistake.

He stepped softly to one side as Deloit's gaze settled on the window facing him. Had the gunslinger come to the conclusion that the central window of the three was the room being occupied by McCallam? He was right. McCallam grunted. Staying clear of the window would be a priority.

Deloit finished the cheroot, flicked the still glowing nub into the snow and headed back to the bar, leaving the batwings to creak eerily behind him.

McCallam lifted the collar of his coat into his neck, tapped the butt of his Colt and crossed to the door. North Bend, he had concluded, was no place to be, whatever the weather. Time had come to saddle up the mare and take his chances heading north, however slow and difficult the going. He had trusted to his luck before. He would trust it again.

The wind attacked him as soon as he reached the street.

* ★ ★

The snow around the area of the livery's working forge had long since melted into the dirt. Now, with the smoke caught on the brisk wind and the newly fuelled coals deepening to a rich red glow, it was one of the few places in North Bend that morning that offered an unquestioning welcome. Come close, it seemed to say, whoever you are.

McCallam did not hesitate. He was in range of the glow, his arms outstretched to the warmth, within minutes of leaving the room above the store.

'Help yourself,' said a voice at his back. 'Name's Barney — just that. Ed Birch's helpin' hand around here when these old bones have a mind to permit it,' he grinned, offering his hand. 'Don't look as how Ed's goin' to be about for a day or so. Said I'd look to the place. Reckon I'll move in for the time bein'. Whole sight warmer than that back-of-town shack of mine.'

He stepped closer to the forge, selected a long poker and rattled it through the glowing coals. He wiped his eyes as the smoke billowed.

'How is Ed?' asked McCallam.

'Frettin' and gettin' mule-headed along of Cupcake in Doc's back parlour. Fine pair they make too. Dollar to a spit they'll be fightin' before sundown!'

McCallam grinned, glanced quickly back to the deserted street, and rubbed the warmth through his hands.

'Kinda stirred things up some since you arrived,' said Barney, delving in his coat pocket for a bandanna to wipe his tired eyes. 'Figured as how you might, minute I set eyes on you. Said to myself, there's a professional if ever I saw one, I said. You've got the look, mister. Saw it in Sam Cleever out Texas way. You ever meet Sam? Mebbe not. He got gunned at Mallory five summers back.' He smacked his lips, replaced the bandanna and clamped a half-smoked cigar between his teeth. 'Same went for

Jackson Chew. He was a gunman to his fingertips. And you know what, I hear as how he died in a whore's bed last winter. She stabbed him by all accounts. Still, no man took him out with a bullet, did they? Nossir. That's the way of it with the professionals, ain't it? You agree, mister?'

'Wouldn't know,' said McCallam, his gaze unmoving on the glowing forge. 'I ain't a professional. I'm no gunman. And I ain't Frank Chater. I'm John McCallam.' He turned his gaze on Barney. 'But no one here believes me. How about you?'

Barney lit the cigar, blew smoke into the swish of the wind. 'Couldn't give a damn who you are, mister. Names don't mean a pan of beans in my book. I see what I see, speak as I find.'

'So you don't believe me?'

Barney examined the tip of the cigar. 'Would it matter either way?' he asked, lifting his eyes in a tight gaze on McCallam's face. 'You're here; you've done what you've done; folk have seen you. So has Chisholm.' He grinned drew smoke from the cigar and released it. 'And now I suppose you're reckonin' on pullin' out. That why you're here? Fella don't normally come to the livery save to fetch his horse.'

'I figured I'd take my chances,' said McCallam carefully.

Barney shrugged. 'Wouldn't be for riskin' it myself, but . . . I guess you've a mind of your own. I can see that, too.' He drew on the cigar again. 'Still, hope you ain't in too big a hurry to leave us. You've got a visitor.'

McCallam frowned. 'Visitor? Where?'

'Back in the stables. Too dangerous to be seen out here. Follow me.'

* * *

McCallam hesitated in the gloom of the stables where only a single lantern flickered at the far end of the building, and waited for Barney's gesture to go ahead.

He edged deep through the thrown

shadows, the timbered bulk of the bays, the tethered mounts, mounds of straw, forks, tools and in one corner, a heap of steaming dung. He patted a mount as he passed; paused, narrowed his eyes and peered into the dark recesses.

Visitor, he pondered — a polite way of saying that the law out of Williamsville had caught up with him? Maybe there had been more of Slater's men back there in the forest. Maybe other lawmen in other towns, other territories, even bounty hunters, had got to hear of his escape. Hell, they had wasted no time! Was he worth the effort in this weather?

He eased on towards the dim glow of the lantern, paused again, waited, listened, peered. Nothing to see. Nothing to hear.

And then there was a soft, almost whispered voice.

'Here, Mr McCallam.'

The woman took a single step from the deepest shadow, and smiled nervously. 'I guessed you'd head this way after what happened back there in the saloon. Can't say I blame you. North Bend can't be that special.' The smile twitched across her lower lip. 'My name's Maisie — Maisie Peach so far as the fellas round here are concerned.'

'Cupcake mentioned you,' grunted McCallam.

The smile flickered again. 'Guess you're wonderin' why I'm here.'

'I'm listenin' if it'll do any good.'

McCallam's gaze settled on the woman's face with its clear blue eyes, neat nose and well-shaped lips. Her hair, falling below the set of her brimmed hat, was yellow; her skin smooth and clean, save where the blue-black of a heavy bruise spread down one side of her neck like a stain. She fingered it as if suddenly aware of his gaze.

'Chisholm's doin?' he asked.

The woman nodded. 'Him and Deloit. They're of a kind. They're scum.' She took a deep breath. 'Like many, I ain't sure who you are,' she began. 'Some say you're here on a deal brokered by Henry Begine and that your real name's Frank Chater. I hear you callin' yourself McCallam.' She shrugged, removed the finger from the bruise and relaxed. 'I'm with Barney — names don't matter.'

Her eyes widened, taking in the light. 'What matters to me, Mr McCallam, is the fate of the girls at the saloon. If somethin' ain't done about Chisholm and his rats soon, we'll all be' — she drew the folds of her heavy coat aside and fumbled with the buttons of the shirt beneath it — 'like this' she murmured, letting the shirt fall open.

13

The cheroot stub burns on Maisie's lower neck and breasts had been inflicted in a purposeful pattern, a precise arrangement of spacing and intensity. Now, some of the burns had begun to cake in the slow and obviously painful process of healing; others were still raw, soft under whatever cream had been applied by Doc Tucker. Whoever had been responsible for the systematic torture had clearly found some sick, deluded pleasure in doing it.

McCallam swallowed. A beading of sweat broke across his brow. His eyes filled with the sight in front of him and the memories of the nights when the guards at the pen had wiled away the hours with their own variations on burning.

'Chisholm again?' he muttered at last.

Maisie closed and buttoned the shirt,

wincing silently at the scrape of cloth across the tender flesh. 'The girls and me had a disagreement with Chisholm, Deloit and the other rat. They broke down our doors, took away the keys and beat the hell out of us for our trouble. I was judged to be the ringleader, so I got singled out for special treatment.'

She snuggled deep into the folds of the heavy coat and blew into her cupped hands. 'I ain't a pretty sight, am I? Too late now for regrettin' what I did. And, damnit, I'd do it again. You bet I would! But meantime, there's the others . . . Fran, May, young Patsy, Sara . . . they ain't deservin' of bein' treated like they are, and now they're real scared they'll finish up like me — burned, scarred for life, out of a job and out of hope.'

Maisie's gaze hardened to an unblinking stare into McCallam's face. 'Unless Chisholm, Deloit and that animal Shard are killed. Unless there's somebody who'll step up to do it.' She paused a moment.

'Will you be that somebody, Mr McCallam? We're kinda countin' on you seein' as how . . . well, not to put too fine a point on it, seein' as how there ain't nobody here with either the stomach or the skill for undertakin' work for what you are mister — a professional.'

'But that's just — ' McCallam halted mid sentence, held now by the woman's eyes, no longer angry and shot with the gleam of hatred, but waiting, fearing the cold dread that he might shake his head, turn away, go saddle his horse and ride out.

'You should get into the warm, ma'am,' he said. 'Weather's closin' down again.'

Maisie simply smiled and tried to hide the smooth flow of the tear down her cheek.

★ ★ ★

'Change your mind?' said Barney, relishing the warmth of the forge as he and McCallam watched Maisie picking

122

her careful way to the back door of Saddles saloon.

McCallam turned his face to the flurrying snow and thickening winter skies. 'T'ain't lookin' good,' he murmured. 'Mebbe I'll wait.'

Barney grunted and rattled the poker through the glowing embers before feeding the fire with fresh logs. 'Maisie show you what them rats did to her?'

McCallam nodded and pulled at the collar of his coat.

'Said she would. She ain't shy. Anyhow, somethin' like that needs to be seen. Takes some swallowin' to reckon another human bein' doin' it.' Barney grunted again and fed a log to the fire. 'She's been waitin' on you arrivin' for days. Her and the others. Stakin' a lot on what you can do. So what are you goin' to do?'

McCallam ran his hands through the warmth of the crackling flames. 'See Doc Tucker. Which way?'

'Far end of town. Down the street, turn left at the timber yard. Doc's house is the old clapboard place back of it.' He paused. 'I'll book your horse in for a week,' he added. 'Goin' to take that long before we see a thaw.'

'A week,' repeated McCallam. 'That should do fine,' he smiled and faded to a blur on the whipping snowfall.

He reached the sprawl of the timber yard without passing or seeing a soul. Outdoor chores had been postponed, it seemed, pending better weather. The only sensible place to be was indoors hugging the warmth of a fire.

Smoke swept like thick gloved fingers through the snowfall. Lights flickered fitfully in windows from where folk watched to see who might be foolish enough, or desperate enough, to be about. But there were few foot-prints in the steadily deepening snow. Who needed to go any place? Best leave the street to its winter silence.

McCallam's progress, however, had been noted with keen interest.

Most folk now knew of his presence in town. He was the fellow who had rescued Cupcake from bushwhackers; the man in the buckskin jacket who had whipped Spreads Shard and settled the score with Deloit. More . . . he was the stranger whom Chisholm now feared. And still more . . . he was, in fact, a famous gunman who had killed, ten, maybe twenty men; who called himself McCallam, but who was really . . . well, no one was quite sure. Point was, he was here, and there could be only one reason for that. Oh, yes, they all knew why he was here.

But he came at a price. Such men always did. They had enemies, and made two for every one killed. And they never worked cheap. So maybe, some said, there was a whole heap of truth in the rumour that McCallam — or whoever he was — was part of a deal hatched by Henry Begine and even the sheriff himself.

Town eyes watched carefully as McCallam reached the timber yard, paused to take his bearings then trudged away to his left.

He was heading for Doc Tucker's, checking on Cupcake and Ed Birch; maybe he would hear of what happened to that bar girl. Real gunmen — professional gunmen — had a nose for sniffing out detail, for getting to know a place and the folk who lived in it. That way they stayed alive and aware of the threat in the shadows.

★ ★ ★

Doc Tucker had his front door open even before McCallam had knocked.

'Saw you comin',' he said, ushering his visitor into the neat front parlour where the flames of a cheery log fire flickered in the rough stone hearth. 'Figured you'd get here sooner or later.' He crossed to a table where two glasses and a bottle of whiskey waited in the glow of a softly primed lantern. 'You seen Maisie?' he asked bluntly, pouring two stiff measures.

McCallam nodded, pleasantly conscious now of the parlour's warmth seeping into his bones.

'Bad business,' Doc continued, handing a drink to McCallam. 'One of the worst I've seen.' He stared into his glass for a moment, swirled the liquid and sank the measure in a single gulp. 'Amazin', ain't it, how low some men will stoop?'

He replaced the glass on the table. 'Anyhow, wanted to thank you for takin' care of Cupcake like you did. You did a good job. He'll be struttin' round the town again in no time. Same goes for Ed Birch. He'll mend fast enough. See for yourself when you're ready. They're in the back room there.' He gestured to a door in the shadowy wall facing McCallam.

'You leavin' town?' asked Doc suddenly, his grey eyes tightening on McCallam's face. 'Or mebbe I shouldn't ask. T'ain't none of my business.' He smiled gently. 'One thing's for sure, weather's goin' to have the last word. Ain't seen a winter as bad as this in North Bend since . . . hell, too far back to recall.'

McCallam drained his glass slowly, relishing the new warmth within him, wondering if he should once again tell his story of the pen, his escape, the cabin, the new identity, the real events leading to his meeting with Cupcake, and now of how he planned to keep riding north, always one step ahead of whoever might be in pursuit of him. Surely, Doc would understand and believe him?

'Whatever you've got in mind,' Doc went on, 'I figure you should know there are those in town — some misguided fools too darned scared to speak their minds — who Chisholm reckons he might have in his pocket. Know what I mean? I'm sure you do. There's always a rat never more than a step away. And I'm speakin' of the human kind.' Doc's eyes twinkled. 'I'm sure I don't have to tell you that this town's a dark place, full of frightened folk. It don't never get light. So watch your back.'

14

The grey light had deepened under the threatening snow-laden skies when McCallam left Doc Tucker's home and made his way back to the room above the store.

His meeting with Cupcake had been brief and came rapidly to the point as the old man hobbled grumpily round Doc's back room with the aid of a stick.

'I hear you've been makin' yourself known around town,' he had said, wincing when he over-reached himself with a step. 'And darn me so you should. What you reckon, eh, Doc? Man of this fella's standin' and reputation shouldn't be for hidin' himself like some half-wit cockroach. Nossir! You face up to 'em, Mr Chater — or are you still insistin' on callin' yourself McCallam? Don't make no odds. Professional gun's a professional gun by anybody's lights.'

He had hobbled on a few more steps, glared at the stick as if about to take it in both hands and snap it in half, and grunted angrily to himself. 'Chisholm figured you yet? I bet he sure as hell ain't, though he'll be listenin' to town talk and, like Doc's warned you, there are folk about who ain't none too fussed whose company they keep for a quiet life. Know what I mean? Course you do, you're a professional.'

For a moment the old man's eyes had gleamed. 'I been tellin' Doc here, and Ed when he's awake, as how I've seen you in action. I mean real action like you showed when you took out them bushwhackin' scum and gunned them no-hope drifters hangin' on our tails. I told 'em — just like it was.' And then his eyes had lit up as if with the fires of cherished memories.

'So I for one ain't got no fears about you showin' Chisholm the way of things. And them sidekicks of his while you're at it. Tell you somethin' else, mister, if you're figurin' on who you're really doin' this for, well, do it for Maisie, eh? Maisie and them gals of hers. I'd personally be well obliged. You hear that, fella? Good. Now get the hell out of here and let me get some rest and sleep along of Ed, who ain't shifted from that chair in a full five hours!'

Another hobble, another wince, a hissed curse and the meeting was over. The last McCallam had heard after he had thanked Doc and was heading for the door was the sound of Cupcake's voice ordering up a log for the fire.

McCallam smiled quietly to himself as he lowered his head against the flurries of snow. There had been no arguing or reasoning with Cupcake and his conviction that the man he had crossed in the pine forest was and would always be Frank Chater. The name McCallam remained a bluff, a decoy to fool Chisholm into thinking —

It was the sudden movement in a window to his left that forced McCallam to step instinctively out of

131

sight into the deepest shadows.

He waited, watching the faint flicker-
ings of light passing, pausing and
passing again across the dirt and
dust-smeared pane of glass. His eyes
narrowed, peered closer. The shack
housing the single window was fit for
nothing save storage. Nobody lived
there, and certainly not in this weather.

The light flickered again, this time
revealing the shape of a face; a man's
face heavy with stubble, a scrub of
black hair plastered across the forehead,
the chin square, the neck thick and
heavy to broad shoulders. No slip of a
fellow, thought McCallam. But where
had he seen him before?

The light faded as it moved to
another part of the building. Silence.
No movements save the steady drift
of snow, swirling where the wind
trapped it between walls and rooftops.
McCallam hunched himself into his
coat, buried his hands deep in his
pockets and shifted his feet against the
numbing cold.

The shack fell into darkness, the window suddenly black and featureless. Had the fellow left, moved out through some back door, or was he, like McCallam, simply waiting? Had he seen McCallam, been watching for him? Why? Who was he? Doc Tucker's words echoed through his thoughts: 'This town's a dark place . . . Watch your back . . . '

He grunted, felt the bulge of his Colt and stepped to the edge of the shadow. The street was still deserted, the lights in windows a warm amber against the darkness and snow. Nobody, it seemed, was about, not even on the boardwalk fronting the saloon.

He had left the shadows and begun the slow trudge in the direction of the store when he became aware of somebody close and moving closer.

Then he heard the click of a gun hammer.

'Easy there, mister.'

McCallam turned slowly, his eyes squinting against the snowfall for a closer look at the man. 'I know you, fella?' he asked.

'Don't have to. I ain't here for a chat. This is strictly business.'

'Business, eh?' McCallam balanced his stance in the snow; felt the weight of the holstered Colt against his thigh. 'You've got a strange way of goin' about it. I ain't much for doin' business on a cold street in the snow, specially when there's a barrel levelled on my gut. You wanna step some place dry and talk this through?'

'You ain't welcome in this town, mister. You ain't wanted,' snapped the man, shifting the gun a fraction in his hurry to spit out the words.

'That you sayin' I ain't wanted, or is that Royce Chisholm puttin' words in your mouth?' McCallam's eyes had narrowed to no more than slits as he peered for a sight of the man's face.

'Most feel the same.'

'That a fact? Can't say I've heard it myself.' McCallam felt again for his balance. Snow cracked under his boot.

His breath swirled ahead like a ghost cloud. 'So what you plannin'? You want I should saddle up and ride? In this weather? Goddamnit, man, I wouldn't inflict that on a horse, would you?'

'You ain't ridin' nowhere, mister. Your ridin' days are — '

The man had probably meant to say 'all through', but he never got to speak the words as McCallam's left boot kicked violently through the snow, spraying a shower across the man's line of vision to give McCallam the few seconds he needed to draw his Colt and loose two fast shots, the second lifting the man off his feet and hurling him back like a bundle of rags.

The roar of the blaze had growled across the gathering dusk to bring two men stumbling from Saddles saloon, a light to blaze into life in Begine's mercantile, Sheriff Hart to fling open the door to his office and for Doc Tucker to come scurrying through the snow, one arm safely into the sleeve of his coat, the other swinging like a pendulum under the weight of his bag.

'What the hell's goin' on here?' shouted Hart, crossing the street through the driving snow. 'Who's been shot?'

'Bart Miller,' called a man, peering at the body. 'He had a gun drawn on McCallam here. Saw it all from across the street. Bart had been waitin' on him in the old shack.'

'That how it happened, McCallam?' asked Hart.

'Just like that.' McCallam holstered his Colt. 'Who is he, f'Chris'sake?'

'One of them I warned you about,' said Doc, clearing snow from the dead man's face as he examined the body. 'And he ain't the only one.'

★   ★   ★

Henry Begine bolted the store door behind him, leaned against it for a moment then crossed through the dimmed lantern light to where Sheriff Hart and McCallam waited in the softer shadows.

'This is gettin' serious,' he said, drawing a bandanna from his pocket to mop his brow in spite of the cold. 'Chisholm's worried. He's mebbe figured who you really are. That fella — Bart Miller, the scumbag — he was one of those in Chisholm's pay. There's others. Six, eight, who knows? They'll do whatever Chisholm orders for bein' left alone and paid whatever pittance he hands out.' Begine swept the bandanna back to his pocket. 'He ain't goin' to like what's happened. No sayin' what he'll do.'

'Mebbe we should've thought of that before hirin' Mr Chater,' murmured the sheriff.

'I ain't Chater and nobody's hired me,' snapped McCallam.

'Too late now whoever you are,' said Hart, raising his eyes to McCallam's face.

McCallam leaned forward into the lantern's weak glow. 'That message you sent,' he said, his stare concentrating on Begine. 'How did you send it? There ain't no telegraph office in North Bend; the wire was dated out of Markfield. How come?'

Begine drew the bandanna again, wiped his face and smiled. 'Simple — as you know. The deal was done out of Markfield by my friend — and a trusted supplier to me over many years — Sam Beadle. Sam recommended you were the man we were lookin' for and said he knew how to contact you in Williamsville. Said it right here in the store. He did all the negotiatin' in my name from there on. But look, we're wastin' time here. Goin' over this ain't servin' no purpose.' He stared hard at McCallam. 'Do your job, Mr Chater, and you'll get your money. Don't doubt it.'

The storekeeper crossed to the store's glass-fronted doors and peered into the street. 'Oh, hell,' he wheezed, swallowing as the sweat broke across his brow. 'Best come and look at what we have here, Mr Chater.'

15

McCallam stared into the suddenly busy street where a flood of lantern lights lit up Saddles saloon, the smoke-hazed bar, the boardwalk and the gathering of townmen wrapped against the biting cold and swirling snowfall.

Standing centre stage was Royce Chisholm, a Winchester in his hand, Deloit prowling at his shoulder like a black hound. Moses Fletcher hovered uncertainly, moving from one spot to another, torn between finding somewhere to hide or making a run for it. He had neither the strength nor courage to do either.

The beanpole barman gazed bemusedly around him, a glass in one hand, a cloth in the other. A couple of bar girls watched anxiously. Portly Mann lurked in the shadows. An old-timer released clouds of smoke from his glowing pipe. A woman with a long scarf squashing her bonnet to her head and covering her ears stared indignantly into Chisholm's face without her eyes appearing to blink. Chisholm seemed not to notice her.

It was some minutes before Chisholm raised a hand and the townfolks' murmurings faded.

'Mr McCallam,' he called across the street, his gaze tight on the store, 'I know you're in there; you, too, Sheriff. Well, now, you just shift your butts, pair of you. I got a proposition. A straight up, no messin' deal. And you got my word in front of all these witnesses — darn near a half of the town — as how there'll be no shootin'. The Good Lord strike me down if I'm lyin'.'

'The Good Lord ain't that generous,' muttered Begine, glancing quickly at McCallam.

'What's the rat schemin' now, f'Chris' sake?' mumbled Hart. 'Chisholm's word is about as reliable as a lame horse.'

A scattering of snowflakes drifted through the lantern glow. The crowd's attention had turned to the store. Moses Fletcher dusted cigar ash from his waistcoat. A bar girl shivered and bit her lip. The staring woman had not shifted her line of concentration in spite of Deloit's carefully aimed fount of spittle that squelched only inches short of her ankle-length skirts.

'You've sure got an annoyin' way of not hearin' a fella, McCallam,' called Chisholm again. 'You want I should repeat myself, or do I have to — '

The door of the store creaked open and McCallam stepped into the street.

'Well, now, that's a whole sight more promisin',' grinned Chisholm. 'You bet. Now if you'll step up here, my friend, you can hear the full detail of my deal down to the last word. That fair enough? I'd reckon so, and I guess most here would agree. So stand aside, folks, make way for the man.'

McCallam did not move. Hart eased slowly from the store to his side. Begine stood in the doorway, sweat beading on his face, the bandanna hanging loose in his hand.

'What's all this about, Chisholm?' said the sheriff. 'This ain't a night for hangin' about in the street.'

Chisholm took a step forward. 'Quite right, it ain't, so let's get this over, shall we? Here's the deal.' He tightened his grip on the Winchester as if signalling that whatever he proposed was not for being negotiated. 'You, McCallam, are leavin'. No arguin'. You ain't welcome here, you ain't needed, and I personally don't like you. Now, you appreciate I could have you shot right now, right where you stand. But I ain't for that. I've got a better way.' He gestured to the shadows to his right. 'Let the fella see for himself,' he grinned, as Barney led McCallam's horse, saddled, blanket roll and side panniers in place, to the foot of the steps fronting the saloon.

The town folk murmured among themselves. Moses Fletcher began to choke on a newly lit cigar. The old-timer's pipe erupted in a cloud of smoke and glowing embers. The woman in the tied-down bonnet closed her eyes and muttered to herself.

'Like I say, McCallam, you're leavin' — tonight. Barney here has prepared your horse; there's blankets and food for a few days, or for as long as you survive out there. By my reckonin' you won't last long. But the odds are a mite better than stayin' where you are.' Chisholm grinned, flexed his grip on the rifle and motioned to Deloit. 'Ease them guns of yours to the ground, McCallam; you too, Sheriff, and that snivellin' storekeeper back of you. That's right, nice and easy, nice and slow. Mr Deloit here will collect them.'

'You're condemnin' this man to his death, Chisholm,' growled Hart. 'Damnit, there ain't nothin' could survive out there, not in these conditions.'

'Do as he says,' murmured McCallam. 'Don't rile him. There's too many folk here. If he gets to usin' that Winchester . . . Just do it, Sheriff. I'll take my chances.'

The townfolk had begun to murmur again, talking among themselves, switching their gazes from Chisholm to McCallam, to Deloit, as he crossed the street to collect the guns.

'Once you've cleared town, McCallam, you keep ridin', any direction you choose. I ain't fussed,' called Chisholm. 'And you keep goin'. You understand? Any attempt you make to return here, any sightin' of you close by, any *rumour* of you comin' back or hangin' about, and these folk will suffer, you got my word on that, and I won't be choosy about who they are: men, women, young 'uns, it don't matter.' His dark expression tightened. 'You keep your side of the deal, McCallam, and I'll hold to mine. Break it . . . You've been warned.' He swept the barrel of the rifle round the gathering of silent, staring townsfolk. 'And so have they.'

★　★　★

144

The whole town, it seemed, watched McCallam cross the street, take the reins to the mount from Barney, and mount up. They watched Chisholm's glare, saw his grip on the rifle begin to twitch; saw the look on McCallam's face. Would he speak? He had no gun, no weapon of any kind. The professional had been stripped to the bare bones. Fast gun he might be; a killer by instinct, a gun for hire, but right now he was nobody, just a fellow being forced to face an almost certain death.

'Goddamnit, might as well shoot the fella now,' murmured the old-timer, the pipe clamped tight between his broken teeth. 'Be a whole sight kinder than turnin' him out to the weather out there.'

'Won't last the night, never mind a day,' murmured a man at his side. Portly Mann, stepped from the shadows. 'Think again, Chisholm,' he began. 'You can't let a man — '

Chisholm swung the barrel of the rifle through a vicious swipe that caught

Portly across the cheek to send him sprawling across the boardwalk, blood pouring from a deep gash. 'Keep out of it if you know what's good for you,' he growled. 'Next time it'll be a bullet.'

'Best go and fetch Doc,' said Hart quietly to Henry Begine. 'Chisholm in this mood might lead to anythin'.'

The townsfolk had begun to back away from the glow of the lights, some still muttering and murmuring, some stunned to a brooding silence by what they had seen and heard. What was happening to them, their town; what might happen in the future? Was there a future? Was it riding out with John McCallam?

'Mare's in good shape,' said Barney, his eyes deep in despair as he watched McCallam take a hold of the reins. 'She won't let you down.' He managed a faint smile. 'And take good care of that bedroll. You're goin' to need it.'

McCallam grunted, mounted up, flexed his fingers through the reins and turned the mount to the west. Minutes later he was no more than a dark blur on the snowfall, then nothing as the swish of the horse's hoofs faded and the night closed in like a mourner's cloak.

* * *

'He's gone! We *let* him go, f'Chris'sake. We just stood there. Never raised a finger. What sort of people are we?'

Henry Begine gazed round the shadowy faces of the men gathered in the dim lantern glow of his store. Outside in the now deserted street, a thin snowfall swirled on the drift of the north wind. Only the lights at the saloon were any sign of life in an otherwise eerily hushed winter's night.

Sheriff Hart paced moodily from one end of the store to the other, turned and addressed the men. 'T'ain't no use thrashin' ourselves over the way things have panned out. We had no choice back there. One move from any one of us would have sparked Chisholm and that louse Deloit into retaliatin' in a

147

manner I ain't for thinkin' of. You heard his threat. He wasn't foolin'.'

'But mebbe we should have at least tried,' quipped a youth with a vast scarf coiled like a snake round his neck.

'Sure,' piped Doc Tucker from a corner of the store where he was tending to Portly Mann's gashed cheek, 'and how many would've finished like Portly here, and mebbe a whole sight worse? In fact, definitely a whole sight worse.' He steadied Portly as he swabbed the wound and applied a dark tincture that stained his cheek to a fiery purple. 'Got to face it, men, Royce Chisholm is for killin' the minute he's crossed. That's the keg of dynamite he truly is, make no mistake.'

'But that wouldn't have troubled Frank Chater,' said Begine, beginning to sweat again. 'You all saw that. You saw the way he handled Shard. The way he stood to Deloit. Damn it, Chater had the measure of Chisholm, and he sure as hell had an edge on the scumbag. That's why he was here; why he was hired. We were payin' him good money.'

'Not any more we ain't,' grunted the old-timer, examining the charred bowl of his bent pipe. 'Assumin' the fella was Chater,' he added ruefully.

'Heck, you ain't still doubtin', are you?' clipped Begine, flourishing his bandanna angrily. ' 'Course the man was Chater. Fact that he was callin' himself McCallam was simply a cover. That was obvious.'

'Don't matter none, anyhow,' muttered a man with a sewn sacking cape covering his shoulders and back. 'Like you say, he's gone, and I wouldn't wager a bean on the fella showin' again. Not no how. And he ain't armed, remember that. If he's got any sense — '

'Well, mebbe we could go track him,' said a man with a bushy pepper-and-salt beard. 'Won't be difficult to pick up his trail. Give it an hour or so and there'll be some light. If we move then — '

'Waste of time, mister,' mused Doc,

putting the finishing touches to Portly's cheek. 'Weather out there is wicked beyond words and likely to stay so for another couple of days. 'Sides, who says the fella, whoever he is, could be persuaded to come back? It's goin' to take all his wits, and a heap of luck, to survive. All he'll be interested in is movin' on.'

'So what do we do?' asked the man huddled in sacking. 'Just sit here, let Chisholm do as he likes, take what he likes, includin' the women? What do you reckon, Sheriff? We goin' to let this happen without a word, same as we let McCallam ride out?'

16

No one could be certain why the silence deepened quite so suddenly in North Bend. Some reckoned it was the snow. 'It muffles everythin',' the old-timer explained. 'And folk don't stray a deal in snow, do they? They stay home, safe with their fires, warmth, home cookin' best they can manage.'

Others swore it was fear. 'T'ain't safe to walk the street, is it?' the bushy bearded man had told a handful of men gathered at the forge. 'Folk are scared. Hell, who knows what mood Chisholm's in when he wakes? One day he'll barely open his mouth; another he's for shootin' up the whole town and anybody who steps across his gun sights. It just don't pay to be about, specially for the womenfolk.'

But others thought the reason for the silence went much deeper. 'It's shame,' said Portly Mann, watching Henry Begine stock his store shelves. 'We shouldn't have let that fella ride out like he did. We should've done somethin' — ain't sure what, but it should've been somethin'. And we should be doin' somethin' now. Anythin' so long as it's somethin'. Mebbe you could raise another hired gun, Henry. Have you thought of that?'

The storekeeper had given his answer in his own deep silence and found another shelf to restock.

For Maisie and the bar girls at Saddles saloon the silence was a threat. It lay there like something waiting to spring into fearful life, or take the shape of Spreads Shard seeking out someone to taunt and abuse; a half-drunk Deloit to avoid if you valued your sanity, and worse, Royce Chisholm in a vengeful mood.

Maisie kept herself to herself whenever possible, recalling her meeting with McCallam in the livery, watching him being forced out of town to face the snowy wastes, but never forgetting the look she had seen in his eyes. That had given her hope — and she was clinging to it.

Moses Fletcher was drifting perilously close to a nervous breakdown as he witnessed his home and his business drawn ever tighter into Chisholm's demanding clutches.

'He'll ruin me. Ruin us all,' he had confided to those few customers who had braved the weather and the hazards of Chisholm's shifts of mood and temper. 'The fella ain't sane, that's for sure. He's mad. And Shard and Deloit along of him. I tell you fellas straight up, no messin, this bar will be runnin' with the blood of men before we're through. And that's fact. Mark my word. Why on earth McCallam didn't shoot the three of 'em when he had the chance I'll never know . . . '

It was a puzzle troubling Sheriff Hart.

'Mebbe I've got it wrong; mebbe I've always had it wrong, but ain't a hired gun a whole heap more intent in laying his hands on the money than he is in playin' around with his quarry?' he had asked Doc Tucker when they sat relishing an early morning coffee in his office. 'McCallam had more than one chance of settlin' matters with Chisholm, so why didn't he take it? What held him back? Is that the way Frank Chater operates?'

'I doubt it,' said Doc bluntly. 'But, then, we wouldn't know, would we? When was the last time we had occasion to welcome a professional gunslinger to North Bend? Not in my time, and probably not in yours. In fact, now you come to mention it, I can't recall ever actually crossin' the path of a hired gun. Only Cupcake appears to have had that privilege, and from what he tells me of McCallam's — or is it Chater's? — abilities with a gun, well, I'd guess there ain't much doubt we had the fella here, right there in our own street.' He had paused behind the drifting steam of the hot coffee. 'Or did we?'

McCallam's fate since riding out on that cold, dark, snow-filled night had continued to fret in the minds of townsfolk. Some could not sleep easy with the thoughts of what might have befallen him out there in the frozen wastelands. Most felt a gnawing sense of guilt. None more so than Halfcase Tibbetts, the man in the sewn-sacking cape.

Halfcase was a loner. He had drifted into North Bend when the town had been no more than a handful of shacks and tents and a trading post. But unlike many others of his kind and calling, Halfcase had stayed until, as he freely admitted, the town had become his home. 'The only one I ever had as I recall,' he had been happy to claim.

What no one had suspected was the fellow's deeper feelings for the place; a sense of security, belonging and love he was ready to fight for, even die for. No 'upstart, gunslingin' scum' were going

155

to take North Bend away from him. Damn it, he would sooner breathe his last defending it than hand it to 'murderin' rats'.

They were exactly Halfcase's thoughts three days after McCallam had been driven from town.

On that morning, the first to dawn without a canopy of snowclouds, with a bright, full-blooded winter sun rising early in the east, Halfcase had taken his rifle from the backroom chest, unwrapped it from its nest of oilcloths and let it rest easy in his hands.

Been an age since he had last fired it, he reflected; not since those youthful days in Evershed when, yes, he had been a fair shot, good enough to settle Johnny Swit the night he found him raping young Jody Jones back of the Bannermans' barn ... But that had been a long, long time ago.

Today was different. This was all about survival, not only for himself, for everyone, for the whole darned town. And facing an all-time gunslinging killer. But somebody had to make a stand; somebody had to do it.

It had taken less than ten minutes for it to be noted that Halfcase was walking down the middle of the street, a rifle in his hand, the gleam of a killing glazing his eyes.

The old-timer, a stream of pipe smoke swirling in his wake, was the first to warn Sheriff Hart. 'Best get yourself out here,' he had called from the boardwalk fronting Hart's office. 'Halfcase is lookin' like he's goin' to settle the world's problems. He's got a real gleam in his eye — and he's got that old rifle of his in his hands. Headin' for the saloon. Only one thing on his mind, if you ask me.'

The old-timer's warning together with the sheriff's appearance, drew Henry Begine from his store, Barney to halt work at the forge and for those townmen about the street to gather in huddled groups.

Halfcase seemed not to notice. He simply trudged on oblivious to the drifts of snow and ice-gripped ruts, his gaze tight on his objective: Royce Chisholm and his sidekicks holed up in Saddles saloon.

'I figure that'll be far enough,' said Hart, brandishing his own rifle when he had got ahead of Halfcase and called to him from the boardwalk outside the old saddlery workshop. 'If you're intent on what I reckon you might be, ain't no good goin' to come of it, fella. This ain't the way.'

'You got a better suggestion, Mr Hart?' sneered Halfcase, taking a fresh grip on his rifle.

'No, can't say I have. But I sure as hell know how this is goin' to end.'

Halfcase stamped his boots in the snow and twitched the sacking cape into his neck. 'So do I. You can bet to it. I've thought it through real close and tidy.'

'I somehow doubt that,' said Hart, watching closely now out of the corner of his eye for any movement at the saloon. 'Why don't you and me talk this through between us? Just you and me, back at my office where it's warm and there's fresh coffee brewin'. Somethin' stronger if you've a mind.'

Halfcase shook his head. 'No, no, no! I'm all through with talkin' and listenin' to talk. I've had talkin till it's like a bad rash. Now I'm scratchin', Sheriff. Oh, yes, I'm scratchin' and puttin' an end to this once and for all. Somethin' we should've done a long time back. So you stand aside there, Mr Hart. Don't mean you no harm nor anybody else who's for a decent, peaceful livin'. This is my business and I'll settle it. Settle it for all of us.'

Halfcase took a step forward.

Sheriff Hart followed suit, this time ranging the rifle clear into Halfcase's gut. 'I ain't for firin' this piece, my friend, but believe me I will if I have to. Now steady up, fella, do like I say and step back with me to my office.'

A townman in the huddle outside Begine's store blew into his frozen hands. 'He's mad,' he said, nodding at

Halfcase. 'Crazed as a sun-struck gopher.'

'He ain't listenin' to the sheriff, that's for sure,' said another.

'Get himself killed if he ain't careful,' clipped a man with a scarf tied over his ears.

'Got some nerve, though, ain't he?' piped a freckle-faced, red-haired youth.

'No brains more like!'

Halfcase moved again, his three steps firm, defiant, steady. 'T'ain't no use you trackin' me like that, Mr Hart. I ain't for bein' put off. 'Sides you wouldn't fire that thing. Not at one of your own, you wouldn't.'

'We've got enough trouble in this town without you addin' to it. Now, for the last time will you — '

The saloon bar 'wings swung open like a black hawk flexing for flight, and creaked back into place behind the shape of Deloit, twin Colts holstered at his waist.

'Well, well, what do we have here?' he grinned, his fingers stretching beneath his leather gloves. 'You lookin' for somebody, mister?'

'Too right I am,' snapped Halfcase, easing a step closer to the saloon boardwalk. 'You for one — and them two-bit friends of yours. I'm lookin' for all of you, every one.'

'You got somethin' specific in mind, fella? You sure as hell look like you're troubled. Winter gettin' to you?'

'Let him be. Deloit,' called the sheriff. 'He's a townman. I can handle him.'

Deloit's grin flickered. 'Sure you can at that, Sheriff. Don't doubt it for a minute, but I got a feelin' our townman here is makin' trouble. Big trouble, like takin' to blazin' with that rifle he's clutchin'. Makes me nervous. It make you nervous? I'm sure them law-abidin' folk gathered back there are nervous.'

'Like I say, you can leave it to me,' said Hart, a cold chill already fingering his spine. 'This is a town matter.'

Deloit spat deep into the snow. 'I

ain't so sure on that score. Nossir. From where I'm standin' — '

'You can save the words, Deloit,' flared Halfcase. 'They don't mean a darn thing. It's somethin' done, I want to see. Somethin' to clear our town of louse and the stink of 'em. Somethin' that buries vermin real deep out of our sight and out of our lives. You get that, mister, 'cus it sure is the sonofabitch truth where you're concerned!'

Deloit's fingers stretched again. His stare seemed to settle like a shaft of light that burned and grew brighter, then dimmed as if to shield his innermost thoughts.

Sheriff Hart swallowed, conscious of a sweat beading on his brow. He could sense what was coming, almost see and hear it before the moment when Deloit's fingers flashed to the Colts, brought them clear of leather and blazed across the thin winter air like flame.

The huddled groups of men stiffened, gasped, blinked and closed their

162

eyes. When they opened them again they saw the sprawled, dead body of Halfcase Tibbetts, his blood staining his sewn sacking like a splash of rich sunlight.

17

'I'm goin'. And I ain't for arguin' the point. Ain't a man here can stop me, so don't let nobody try. I started this, now I'm for finishin' it.'

Sheriff Hart, Doc Tucker, Portly Mann, the old-timer, the man with a pepper-and-salt beard, and a group of others watched in chilled silence at the back of the store as Henry Begine put the finishing touches to the items he would need on the long ride ahead of him.

'And just where do you think you're goin'?' asked Doc, in as calm a tone as he could summon between bewilderment and the biting cold of the north wind.

'Williamsville,' said Begine, checking the packing of a spare coat and boots.

'You'll never make it,' quipped the old-timer, lighting his pipe against the swirl of the wind. 'Not a hope.'

Begine swung round to face the men. 'Look, what we've just witnessed out there, the cold-blooded murder — can't call it other — of Halfcase Tibbetts, is only a start. We know it's only a start. There ain't nobody to stand to them scum, is there? So what'll they do? They'll go on killin' as they please. At random. Anybody in their way whose face don't fit, or says the wrong thing. And it won't just be the likes of us. How long before they get to work on the girls again? Tonight, tomorrow, two days, a week? Who's to say? Nobody can say. And there's nobody to do a darn thing about it. We need a gun. A hired gun. A professional. We need Frank Chater.'

'We had Frank Chater, f'Chris'sake,' snapped Doc. 'Had him right here in North Bend. Or so we believed. Look what happened? You don't imagine he'll be back do you? Chances are he ain't even alive. All you'll find out there is a dead body — *very* dead and *very* frozen.'

'Doc's right,' piped a townman. 'Chater won't have lived. Can't have. But even if he did — and that'd be a miracle — he wouldn't be for settin' his sights on North Bend again, would he?' The other men nodded and murmured their agreement, their breath swirling round them.

'I don't agree,' said Begine. 'If Chater's alive, he'll be back. We had a deal. A good deal, and he won't be for walkin' out on it. T'ain't professional. But if Chater ain't alive, if all I find out there is a body, then I'll push on to Williamsville. I'll find a gun there, sure enough. It's the sort of place the professionals look for business. Don't worry, I shan't let you down. I'll be back — and I'll have company.'

'Then let someone ride with you,' urged the sheriff. 'You can't go alone, not in these conditions. It's too dangerous, too risky.'

'No more arguin',' said the store-keeper, patting his mount's neck. 'Portly here will run the business for me. Store won't close. And if Chisholm gets curious, if he should ask for me, tell him the truth. Tell him where I've gone and tell him why. He'll mebbe get to sweatin' on the prospect!'

★　★　★

'What time is it'?' winced Cupcake, hobbling from the table in Doc Tucker's front parlour to the window overlooking the dark buildings of the snow-dense, silent end of town.

'Five past,' said Doc, shifting the papers arranged on his knee where he sat in the comfortable leather chair.

'Five past what?' croaked Cupcake, through another wince.

'Five past any hour you choose, my friend,' smiled Doc to himself. 'It don't make no odds where you're concerned. You ain't goin' no place'.

'I know that, damnit,' snapped

167

Cupcake. 'Wish I could. Wish I could be out there right now along of Mr Begine. He could use somebody like me.' He stared into the grey light beyond the room.

The sun of the early day had long since dimmed to a smudge and then faded completely behind the gathering snow clouds. The wind whipped, darted through gaps, around corners, tormented loose boards, swinging signs, whined through crannies, skimmed the snow surfaces as if breathing across them.

Cupcake grunted to himself and tapped the tip of his walking stick against his boot. 'He'll have made five miles by now,' he said, staring into the grey space. 'Not much more, not if he's taken the side trail flanking Crow's Outcrop and headed due west for Ten Pines Pass.'

'That the way you'd go if you were out there?' asked Doc, shuffling the papers.

'Too right I would. Only way to go

when the snows close in. He could be out of Ten Pines and making for the forest before the light's done — what there is of it.'

Doc slumped back in the chair, and sighed. 'We shouldn't have let him go. Didn't make sense then; doesn't make sense now. Fella out there, in this weather, alone . . . McCallam had no choice. He had to leave — or face a bullet. But Henry . . . ' He closed his eyes. 'Still, typical of this town right now, ain't it? Things happen, and for some reason best known to ourselves, we simply stand back and let them. Chisholm, McCallam, Halfcase, Maisie, Ed, yourself; now Henry . . . ' He opened his eyes tiredly. 'Who's next? What's next?'

Cupcake peered closer into the grey light as he leaned towards the window. 'Well, I wouldn't really know Doc,' he said slowly, 'but somethin' is. Portly's makin' his way here, and in some hurry. Now what in tarnation's whipped him into a lather?'

★　★　★

Portly Mann took the generous measure of whiskey from Doc in his blue-cold hands, sipped at it, smacked his lips and murmured a grateful 'thanks' through chapped lips.

'Tell us again,' said Doc, watching the man carefully. 'In your own time. No rush.'

Portly took another sip of the drink before finishing it in a single gulp. 'That's a whole sight better, Doc,' he grinned, conscious for a moment of the melting snow from his boots forming in pools at his feet. 'Sorry about the — ' He began, only for Doc to raise a hand and shake his head dismissively.

'Get to what you have to say, Portly,' he said. 'Weather's of no consequence.'

Portly placed the empty glass on the table. 'You could've blown me out like a feather. Couldn't believe my eyes. There he was, large as life, just standin' there, a sort of dazed look in his eyes like he'd seen a ghost or somethin'.' He swallowed. 'Henry, I says, Henry, what's happened, f'Chris'sake? How come you're back? Weather get to you? Trail blocked? You feelin' all right?

'He just stood there, hell, must've been close on a minute. Seemed like it, anyhow. Then he shows me somethin' he's been holdin' behind his back. A hat. Stiff, frozen near solid.' Portly swallowed again. 'McCallam's hat. No doubt about it.'

'Sonofa-goddamn-bitch,' muttered Cupcake under his breath.

'You're sure the hat's McCallam's?' said Doc.

'Too right I'm sure,' nodded Portly, flinching at the throb from his wound as he placed the hat on the table. 'Seen it on the fella whenever he was about. No mistakin' it. Same goes for Henry. He ain't mistaken neither. Recognized it the minute he saw it.'

'Where'd he find it?' asked Cupcake.

'Says he saw it lyin' there in the snow soon as he hit Crow's Outcrop. Shook him somethin' rigid. I mean, damnit, I'd have felt the same been me out there. Proves only one thing, though, don't it? Can't be no other.'

'And what's that?' said Doc.

'McCallam's dead, ain't he? Gotta be.' Portly slid a shaking finger down the side of his wound. 'Fella don't throw down his hat deliberate, does he? 'Course he don't, specially in this weather.'

'So where's the rest of him?' frowned Cupcake, easing his weight to the support of the stick.

'Asked that very question of Henry himself,' said Portly. 'And he reckons there's no doubt to that neither. He's been eaten. Dragged away by animals — wild dog mebbe — and eaten. Animals can get pretty desperate this time of year.'

'Where's Henry now?' asked Doc.

'At the store. Sheriff Hart was with Barney at the livery when Henry rode back to town. Barney looked to his horse. Mr Hart brought Henry back to the store. He's still with him.'

'Anybody see them — Chisholm or one of his guns?'

'Mr Hart reckons not.'

Doc grunted, took the hat from the table, turned it through his fingers for a moment, then grunted again. 'Henry abandoned thoughts of goin' on to Williamsville?'

'I reckon so. Findin' the hat has sure shook him up some. That and the conditions out there. I don't figure him havin' the stomach for another try, not till the snows ease, anyhow. If we survive that long.'

*   *   *

Royce Chisholm stared through the smoke-hazed gloom of the saloon bar at the man known through town as the Gopher.

The fellow was lean and wiry with bulging eyes and wet, cracked lips; an anxious, nervy man, turning his hat rhythmically through his skinny fingers.

'You sure about this?' said Chisholm, his glare darkening. 'Absolutely sure? 'Cus if you ain't — '

'You got my word on it, Mr Chisholm,' gulped the Gopher, turning the hat faster. 'I ain't never let you down yet. What goes on in this town you get to hear of minute it's happened. You bet. And I was there, Mr Chisholm, right there in the livery, back of the stables, though o'course Barney didn't know to it on account of him bein' all beamy-eyed at the sight of Begine ridin' in with that hat. Then Sheriff Hart turns up and I kinda slid away all soft and silent like I'm good at. You know that, Mr Chisholm. You've seen me operatin'.'

Chisholm sat forward in his chair at the corner table, poured himself a drink from a half-empty bottle, and sat back again. 'I seen you and, yeah, you've got a way with you, but this hat is serious business. Real serious. You appreciate what I'm sayin' here, fella? You're sure it was McCallam's hat you saw?'

174

'On the grave of my long since departed grandpapa, Mr Chisholm, I swear that was McCallam's hat in Henry Begine's hand. No mistakin' it. I reckon that storekeeper had ridden out lookin' for the fella, eh, Mr Chisholm? You reckon that? Mebbe he ain't to be trusted. Mebbe I should keep an eye on him. Shall I do that, Mr Chisholm?'

The Gopher blinked over his bulging eyes. His wet lips broke to a quivering grin. Water beaded bright as stars in his stubble.

'You do that, fella. You do just that,' said Chisholm, leaning forward again. 'Meantime have a drink, then get yourself out of here. Go earn your miserable keep.'

'You got it, Mr Chisholm. Just like you say,' beamed the Gopher, showing a full set of tobacco-stained teeth.

Later, when the man had scurried away to the deserted street, Royce Chisholm and a morose looking Deloit sat alone at the corner table, a fresh bottle of whiskey and two clean glasses between them.

'Hell, man, cheer up some, will you?' grinned Chisholm. 'We've had some good news, ain't we? That McCallam burr is out of our boots. We ain't goin' to be troubled by him again, are we? Nossir. Like as not he's all bones out there by now. Nothin' of him left.'

'Yeah, and that's the trouble of it, ain't it?' said Deloit, moodily, turning an empty glass through circles in front of him. 'That's the whole trouble, damnit! Who was he? We still don't know, do we?'

Chisholm helped himself to a generous measure. 'You want to know my thinkin' on it, my friend? I'll tell you. I reckon McCallam was a drifter, simple as that. A no-hoper down on his luck who struck North Bend by accident. He was a nobody. True, he might once have been somebody, but not any more. No, somewhere down the line he'd lost it, had it taken from him . . . Hell, who knows? Fact is, he ain't here and we are. And that, in my book, is good enough. So drink to our good fortune, friend. We have a town, a whole town, in our hands. How about that?'

'Yeah, later mebbe,' said Deloit, coming to his feet to cross to the batwings and the sight of the bleak street beyond them. He hated winter, he thought. Hated it.

Winter was a time for ghosts.

18

The hauntings began the following day.

Henry Begine was the first to suffer. His short-lived journey into the snowy wastelands, the startling discovery of McCallam's hat and the thoughts of the grisly end the fellow might have met, had left him nervy and uncertain of the future — if indeed there would be one.

Sleep had not come easy. He had drifted through what little there had been of it in bouts of sudden sweats, then chills, frightening images of Chisholm and his sidekicks, the mutilated body of Maisie Peach, the deserted street, the snowfall red with the blood of dead men . . .

But on this night Henry had been woken by a sound.

It had come from somewhere in the store beneath his living quarters. Had it been a footfall, the sound of something being disturbed, lifted, dropped? Or was the store cat getting clumsy in his old age?

He had lain awake for some minutes before summoning the courage to leave the warm bed, light a lantern and make his slow, careful way down the bare wooden stairs to the side door that led to the store.

He winced at the creak of the door as it opened to his touch. He held the light ahead of him, its flickering glow throwing thick shadows across the counter, the piles of goods, the stacked shelves, the swept floor, the gleam of polished boards.

It had taken two deep breaths and the creep of the night cold to spur him on. Nothing at first glance appeared to have been disturbed. He held the lantern higher, called the cat's name, glanced at the locked and bolted door to the street, ran a dust-searching finger out of habit along the counter. Nothing.

He had half turned to return to the warm bed when for some inexplicable reason he began counting blankets.

There had been eight in the pile at the far end of the counter. Three blue blankets; two green; one black; two brown. There were only six blankets in the pile now: the brown blankets were missing.

Of course, Portly Mann might have sold them in his absence. But he doubted it. Portly would have said. So somebody had somehow broken into the store — that had to be the sound he had heard — and taken them. Who? Why?

A darker, more chilling thought occurred to him at that moment, one that had sent him hurrying from the store back to the wooden stairs and his living room, the lantern light dancing round him like a shimmer of frantic moths.

*   *   *

At the town livery, Barney's lantern had been burning for more than an hour when he finally discovered where his visiting ghost had spent the better part of the freezing night.

The stabled horses had been spooked on and off since the last of the daylight. None of the dozen or more had seemed to want to settle. They had tended to paw and snort more than usual. The slightest noise roused them. Silence was not to be trusted.

Barney had moved among them, soothing and murmuring, patting those of a particularly nervous nature, making sure they knew he was there, that they were not alone.

He had eventually snatched a couple of hours' fitful sleep, only to be disturbed by louder snorting, more persistent pawing and what he could smell to be an air of growing panic among the mounts.

A closer inspection, once he had calmed the horses again, at first revealed nothing: no intruders, no unusual sounds or movements. But there was a vacant stall at the back of the long block of stabling, and it was here that Barney discovered what he was beginning to half suspect and dreaded finding: somebody had slept in the stall — and not long back.

This, he decided quickly, was a matter for Sheriff Hart.

★ ★ ★

Deloit had avoided the dark for most of the night. It made him feel uncomfortable, and it looked dangerous. It might contain anything; perhaps something that had crept in. Or somebody.

He had let Chisholm drink himself into slumbering oblivion at the corner table. Moses Fletcher had dimmed the lights behind the bar, but known better than to douse them completely. The bar girls had retired to silent rooms. Some would sleep. Some not.

Spreads Shard was keeping himself to himself in his own private room. He was still nursing bruised limbs and joints, not to mention sorely wounded pride. He had resented the news of the likelihood that McCallam had perished in the snow. It had robbed him of plotting his revenge, of how he might soon be taking the sonofabitch apart, limb from limb, slowly, painfully . . . Now, he had only the room, the freezing cold, the window overlooking an empty street.

He needed action, and he would have it, he resolved, come first light.

Meantime, Deloit paced carefully from lantern glow to batwings; back again; paused, turned, renewed the pace, his thoughts gathering like the grey winter clouds.

Suppose McCallam had not died. Suppose he had simply lost his hat. Suppose he had not ridden on. Suppose he was still alive.

Chisholm was always too ready to accept that the fellow had died. But then Chisholm was always too ready to side with the version of anything that played to his advantage. And a whole sight too ready to let Deloit clean up the mess when it all went violently wrong.

But not this time. Nossir. This time Deloit would trust to his own instincts, be a step ahead. Just as soon as it was light . . .

★ ★ ★

The Gopher was true to his word. He had left the saloon well satisfied with his meeting with Chisholm and firmly resolved to continue to serve him. It made good sense. He was proving his worth to the gunslinger exactly as he had planned from the minute Chisholm and his sidekicks had ridden into town.

There were some men you were prepared to cross, some you would be a fool to try. Chisholm was definitely one of the latter. A whole sight better to go along with him, even join him if necessary. That way you stayed alive.

Oh, yes, the Gopher was well satisfied, sure enough. Chisholm trusted him, listened to him — and now, like it or not, was beginning to need him. Who else among the townmen would be such a reliable pair of eyes only too willing to watch, to note, record? Who else had his ear as close to the group as the Gopher? His fellow men could think of him what they liked, call him whatever they chose, but come the day of the final reckoning and Chisholm finally rid himself of Sheriff Hart — and one or two other so-called 'civic-minded' elders — it would be the Gopher who would be standing at the big man's side. You could bet to it.

He was never mistaken where men of Chisholm's kind were concerned. He could read them. Sense their every next thought like he was sitting right there at the back of the fellow's mind. Anticipation, that was the key. The ability to know and understand what a fellow needed, some-times before he knew it himself.

And right now Chisholm's needs were clear enough.

McCallam's presence in town had

undoubtedly troubled him, but now, with the discovery of the man's hat and the near certainty that the fellow had perished, he was feeling a whole lot more relaxed. Now all he needed to bother himself with were the townmen, particularly Henry Begine.

Where had the storekeeper planned to ride? Who had he been hoping to meet: someone to challenge Chisholm?

Well, if that were the case, the Gopher would find out — and soon. Best not to keep a man like Chisholm waiting too long.

The Gopher hurried from the saloon, pulling the collar of his coat high into his neck, passing into and out of the deepest shadows as he crossed the street and disappeared down the alley flanking Begine's mercantile.

There was a back door to the store which Henry was in the habit of forgetting to lock. If that were the case tonight, then the Gopher would be through the door and into the premises in the blinking of an eye. You bet. Who knows, there was maybe something in there that might give a clue to what Begine was planning. He tended to sleep heavy, especially under the warmth of heavy blankets on a winter's night, so there would be ample time to probe around. With any luck the Gopher would be back in the saloon fronting Chisholm with the truth of Henry Begine's trip into the snowlands before first light.

The snowfall had drifted and a high moon gleamed like an eye in the flat black sky when he heard the noise and saw the vaguest shape of a figure to his right.

It seemed to be waiting for him.

19

The Gopher peered into the darkness like an alarmed owl. Who or what is that, he wondered, gulping against the night cold? A drifter, down on his luck? He sure looked it, dressed in what appeared to be rags and blankets, one covering his head and tied under his chin. He was no one he knew. Anybody seen around town dressed like that would not go unnoticed.

So who was he? Where had he come from? What did he want? And why was he standing there like that? Hell, he could be frozen to the spot. Maybe he was. But he was far from dead. He was staring, his eyes shifting at the slightest movement. How long had he been there? More to the point, who was he waiting for?

'Who is that?' hissed the Gopher, not daring to move. 'You want somethin', mister? Looking for somebody?'

No answer. The man continued to stare, his face drained and expressionless.

'If you're lookin' for Henry, he'll be sleepin' tight by now, I'd guess,' said the Gopher wondering now if he might risk a step forward for a clearer view of the man. 'T'ain't no night for standin' about, that's for sure,' he added through the slightest grin.

'So who are you?' said the man suddenly, in a low, cracked voice.

The Gopher stiffened. 'I got business hereabouts,' he snapped. 'I'm a townman. Who are you?'

The man remained silent.

'Look,' said the Gopher irritably, 'if it's somewhere warm and dry you're in need of — '

'I ain't,' snapped the man. 'Are you?'

''Course I ain't. I live here, damnit! I doubt if you do, judgin' by the look of you. Hell, how'd you manage — ?'

'You workin' for Chisholm?'

'I don't see that's any of your

business,' snorted the Gopher. 'Who the hell do you think you are anyway, standin' there like — ?'

'You get a message to him — now, tonight?'

'Well, I don't know about ... ' fumbled the Gopher. He paused. 'I might,' he said, 'if it's that important. But if it's a case — '

'Just tell him I'm back.'

'Who? Who's back?'

'McCallam.'

★   ★   ★

The warmth in Sheriff Hart's office had thickened until the window was a blank under the heat-haze and the smoke from Henry Begine's cigar hanging like a long cloud.

'I ain't mistaken,' the storekeeper repeated for the fourth time. 'I know I ain't. I know my store, every inch of it, and every item of stock I'm carryin'. Only good business, ain't it? So, no, I ain't mistaken. He's come back. Don't

190

ask me why. I don't know. But I do
know he's here.'

'You're right,' nodded Barney, leaning against the wall by the door. 'It's
gotta be him. Who else would want to
sleep in a stable? And you're right on
another count, Henry: we don't know
why. But can we make a fair guess?
Dare we?'

Doc Tucker finished a measure of
whiskey and replaced the glass on the
sheriff's desk. 'Hold on there,' he
cautioned, 'let's not be in any haste.
Even if McCallam is back, it ain't to say
he's returned to settle matters with
Chisholm. He ain't armed to begin
with.'

'Yet,' quipped Begine, with a sly wink
at Barney. 'If he wants a gun, he'll get a
gun. Damnit, I'd give him one myself if
he showed his face!'

'Be careful, Henry,' said the sheriff,
swinging his legs from his desk as he
pushed himself up in his chair. 'I ain't
for havin' any more wild guns around
town. I've got enough with Chisholm

191

and his boys. If McCallam has come back — and I'm inclined to agree that he has — then I just hope you'll let me deal with him. It ain't goin' to take much to send North Bend into a spin that'll end only one way — in a bloodbath.'

'I'm with the sheriff here,' agreed Doc. 'If McCallam's come through his time out there and he's back in town, first thing he's goin' to need is proper shelter, a decent bed for the night, food and warmth. What we can't afford to do is let him loose on Chisholm to go his own way. Assumin' he wants to.'

'Of course he does,' scoffed Henry drawing heavily on his cigar. He released a spiral of smoke. 'He's Frank Chater, ain't he? He's a professional. A gunfighter. Gunfighters don't walk away, and neither will he.' He drew and blew more smoke. 'Money's waitin' on him, just like we agreed. All he's got to do — '

'Yeah, yeah, we've heard all that,' said Hart pouring himself a measure from the bottle on his desk. 'First thing to do here is find the fella. We need to talk to him — serious talk — and hear what he's got to say.'

Barney pushed himself from the wall, crossed to the window and rubbed the pane clear. 'Ain't goin' to get far on that score till first light, are we? Mebbe McCallam will come to us. Or mebbe . . . ' He leaned closer to the window and narrowed his eyes. 'Well, well, look who's about at this hour — the Gopher. Now why ain't he gettin' his beauty sleep, I wonder?'

Sheriff Hart sprang to his feet. 'Let's find out, shall we?' he said, reaching for his heavy coat.

★ ★ ★

They bundled the Gopher from the street to the back room of the store in a flurry of scrambling limbs, swirling scarves and coats.

'What the devil — ?' spluttered the Gopher, pulling himself clear of the grip of Sheriff Hart as a light grew slowly from a primed lantern. 'This is an outrage! It's the middle of the night, f'Chris'sake. And I'm a straight-livin' resident of this town. I've got a right — '

'We all know what brings you out in the middle of the night,' grinned Barney, bringing the lantern to the table in the middle of the cluttered, dusty room. 'And it ain't your concern for the well-bein' of the township.'

'You bet it ain't,' sneered Begine, brushing the stragglings of a cobweb from his coat. 'What you up to now, Gopher? What louse-ridden scheme you dealin' now, eh?'

'All right, Henry, I'll handle this,' said the sheriff, turning a cold gaze on the Gopher. 'We ain't fools, mister. We know darn well you're dealin' with Chisholm. It's what you do, ain't it? It's how you survive, though God knows how you sleep at nights. But that ain't my concern right now. I'm a whole sight more interested in what keeps you out at this Godforsaken hour. And don't tell me to mind my own business. When you're involved, fella, you *are* my business. So — you lookin' for somebody; waitin' on somebody; deliverin' a message? Just what are you doin'?'

Doc Tucker stepped closer to the pool of light as the men's eyes settled tight on the Gopher. 'I wouldn't wriggle like you usually do,' he said, the merest hint of a smile flitting across his lips. 'Get on with it. Time's at a premium in this town right now. We ain't for wastin' it.'

The Gopher shrugged his coat across his shoulders, his gaze shifting jerkily from face to face, the softest smear of sweat beginning to glisten on his brow. 'You ain't got no right,' he began. 'Not one of you. This is supposed to be a free — '

'Now!' barked the sheriff. 'I want to hear the truth right now. No messin'.'

The Gopher swallowed, glanced nervously into the shadows, across the piles of stock, barrels, crates, sacking bales, loose timbers, pick handles. He wiped the back of his hand across his mouth. 'There's mebbe somethin' you don't know,' he said carefully, as if watching each word take shape. 'Somethin' Chisholm don't know yet neither. It concerns that fella McCallam.'

Doc grunted. Begine gripped the lapels of his coat and tightened his gaze. Barney's eyes narrowed.

'Go on,' said the sheriff.

'I told Chisholm about the hat,' the Gopher continued. 'I was at the livery when Henry rode in with it. I saw it all. Chisholm thinks McCallam's dead. But he ain't. He's alive. Here in town. He ain't in very good condition. Not surprisin'. But he's here. Spoke to him not long back. Gave me a message for Chisholm. Said as how I was to tell him he was back.'

'Just that?' said Hart.

'Nothin' else. Then he kinda melted away. Ain't seen him since.'

Doc grunted again. 'So where the hell's he holin' up?'

'Mebbe he's over my place again,' murmured Barney.

'Well, he ain't here, that's for sure,' said Begine, crossing to the room's small, dusty window. 'And I'd doubt if he's out there just waitin'.'

'He's got to be found,' said Doc flatly. 'We just can't have him — '

The single shot blazed and whined across the silent night like a spit of vicious flame.

★   ★   ★

'Douse that light!' Sheriff Hart drew his Colt instinctively as the lantern glow faded. He strode to the window. 'See anythin'?' he murmured at Begine's shoulder.

'Not yet,' said the storekeeper, squinting. He pressed closer to the dusty pane. 'Can't see a deal of the street from here. Hard to make out anything'.'

'Mebbe it'll be better if I go take a look,' offered Barney, moving carefully to the door.

'No, wait,' said Hart. 'This is my job. You stay here and don't move till I give the word.'

Another shot rang out, spitting, whining before fading to an echo through the night's thin air.

'Go easy,' warned Doc. 'Sounds to me like we might have a gun-happy crazy out there.'

The sheriff slid away from the storeroom as soft as a fleeting shadow. He caught his breath at the sting of the cold, felt his eyes begin to water, took a step and stumbled on the packed snow. 'Hell!' he cursed, regaining his balance and peering ahead to the street.

Lights were still burning in Saddles saloon where he could make out the silhouetted shape of Deloit at the batwings. A townman with a lantern held high came from the direction of the smoking forge; another joined him from a side alley; a third, his face muffled in a thick scarf, hurried after them.

'Hell!' cursed Hart again. Only a

matter of time now before half the town was roused and gathering to see who had taken it into his head to shoot up the street in the middle of the night.

He moved on, conscious of each foothold on the frozen snow, his eyes scanning rapidly for the merest hint of the gunman. Nothing, save the bulks of the buildings, the snow-heavy roofs, blank black windows, scuffed tracks pitting the street.

The three men reached the saloon and halted at the sight of Deloit.

'What's goin' on?' asked one of the men, tightening the scarf at his neck.

Deloit simply stared, spat, shifted his stance and drummed his fingers across the butt of his Colt.

'Somebody in a fight?' mumbled the man, with the scarf-muffled face.

Deloit spat again. 'T'ain't none of your business. Get back to your beds.'

'No chance of sleepin' in this town,' grumbled the first man.

A third shot cracked; a fourth. The

sheriff turned sharply. There, some-where at the back of him, no more than yards away.

He saw the bulk of Spreads Shard looming out of the darkness like a black cloud, a Colt tight in one hand, a Winchester clutched in the other. The man's face gleamed with the sweat of wild excitement and anticipation, his eyes dancing in his head like bright swing-ing lights. Boozed or mad, wondered Hart? Probably a deadly combination of both.

'Hell!' he mouthed once again, stepping directly into Shard's path as the man lumbered towards him.

20

Sheriff Hart stood perfectly still, his gaze concentrated on Shard, his right hand flexing slowly, carefully over the butt of his holstered Colt. A thin trickle of sweat broke across his top lip. The darkness seemed to thicken, the shadows to stand like enthralled onlookers.

'That'll be far enough, Shard,' he called, his breath swirling in a wispy white cloud. 'Middle of the night ain't the time for the likes of this, so you just ease them guns to the boardwalk there side of you, and we'll say no more about it. You should be back in the saloon enjoyin' its comforts.' He steadied his gaze on Shard's face, watching every pulse, the shifts of his round, bulging eyes.

'To hell with you, lawman,' growled Shard, staggering to a standstill, sweat gleaming on his stubble, the Winchester probing ahead of him like a hunting limb. 'Time we had some action round here. Place's gettin' stale. Folks are gettin' stale. You're gettin' stale, damnit!'

'Mebbe,' counselled Hart. 'But like I say middle of the night ain't the time. Folk hereabouts are tryin' to get some sleep.'

'Then it's time we woke 'em up, ain't it?' He released three shots from the Winchester, whooping at the top of his voice as each echo climbed, hung on the night then faded. 'You bet! Time the folk of North Bend stirred their lazy butts. Yessir!' He drew the Colt and blazed two shots to within inches of the sheriff's boots.

Hart struggled to hide the flinch that made him blink and shift a leg instinctively against the blast. 'Lay them pieces aside, mister,' he ordered. The trickle of sweat thickened. The cold air seemed to burn like hot embers on his cheeks. 'Do it now before you get to doin' somethin' you're goin' to regret.'

The three men outside the saloon

eased away to the shelter of the street buildings. 'He's in a mood to shoot the town to shreds,' murmured one of them, twirling his scarf round his neck.

Moses Fletcher appeared at the batwings, a cloud of smoke trailing behind him like a stream of grey gulls. He glanced at Deloit, then at the skulking townmen, the street and the dark figures of the sheriff and Shard, feet planted firm in the snow, their gazes fixed and focused.

Trouble, he thought, with a shiver. He could smell trouble. Came with the saloon business. He glanced at the bar clock. Another couple of hours, damnit, and first light would be breaking. Where was Doc? Where were Portly and Begine? He swallowed. Shame about McCallam. Pity Henry found the hat . . .

He turned as Chisholm stirred from his booze-hazed stupor. Trouble. He could smell it creeping up on him right now.

'You goin' to stand aside, Sheriff, and

let a fella get to the business he's about, or have I got to shift you?' Shard waved the Winchester wildly, swayed, threatened to fall, regained an uncertain balance and glared at Hart through steadily reddening eyes.

'I'm still the law in this town, Shard. Don't you go forgettin' it.' The sheriff tensed. 'Now for the last time, are you — ?'

The shot from Shard's Colt blazed with a speed and ferocity that threw Hart from his stance and toppled him to the packed snow. He cursed, scrambled to regain his feet but took another shot that skimmed across his upper arm, tearing his coat and shirt and burning across his flesh like the scorch of a red-hot poker.

'Finish it, Spreads,' yelled Chisholm, reeling through the saloon bar 'wings. 'We don't need a lawman in this town. I'm the law! Finish him!'

Deloit stepped from the boardwalk to the street, his fingers flexing and dancing across the butts of his Colts.

Moses Fletcher moaned, fumbled in a pocket for a cigar, found a blackened stub and tried unsuccessfully to light it.

The three townmen craned necks and bodies from the shadows for a better view of the action. 'Shard'll kill him,' groaned the man with the scarf covering his face. 'Sheriff's a dead man.'

Chisholm ran a hand over his sleep-drawn face. 'Do it, Spreads, f'Chris'sake. Do it now!' he yelled again, staggering perilously close to the edge of the boardwalk.

Sheriff Hart saw the levelled barrel of the Winchester steady on its target. He had no chance, he thought, but wondered if he might still manage to get —

Shard hesitated, a sudden tight, staring look glazing his eyes. His hold on the Winchester weakened until the fingers were sliding away from their grip like poisoned slugs. His mouth opened; a sound began, choked and was swallowed as Shard stumbled forwards, his legs buckling, boots slipping across the snow in opposite directions to the slump of his bulk.

Hart gazed in amazement. What the hell . . . ? Why had Shard hesitated? What was happening to him now? He heard Chisholm's shouts from the boardwalk, was conscious of Deloit straddling the snow, of Doc Tucker, Henry Begine, Barney and the Gopher appearing at the corner of the alley, and then of Shard's final crash facedown in the snow and the gleam of a blade buried in his back.

★   ★   ★

'Where'd it come from? Who threw it, f'Chris'sake?'

Barney cupped his hands and blew into them. 'Hell,' he added through the funnel of cold flesh, 'it came from nowhere.'

'Never saw a thing,' nodded Henry Begine, adjusting the lantern's glow to spread a brighter light through the backroom of the store. He smiled softly. 'Not a thing ... But I know well enough who threw it. Oh, yes, I know that like I know my own hand.' His eyes twinkled. 'It was Frank Chater out there. He threw the knife. 'Course he did. He's here, ain't he? We reckoned we knew that. Now it's for certain, ain't it? Chater's keepin' his promise to the deal. He's goin' to finish the job, just like we planned.'

'Now hold on there, Henry,' cautioned Barney, gazing intently through the glow of yellow light. 'There was somebody there, had to be. Somebody threw the knife and, yes, I grant you it was more than likely McCallam — '

'Chater.'

'All right, Chater. Have it your way. But that ain't to say the fella's goin' to do as you say. He might — '

Begine held up a hand. 'Think back, Barney, think back. Chisholm set great store on sendin' Chater out of town without a gun. He didn't check for a blade. He didn't know that Frank

Chater has a big reputation when it comes to handling a knife. Definitely. I read about it in one of them Eastern newspapers. You bet I did, and I can tell you — '

'Yeah, yeah, I'm sure,' said Barney. 'Ain't doubtin' it, and you may well be right — probably are — but have you thought, Henry, to what this killin' is goin' to mean? Have you reckoned on Chisholm's mood, how he's goin' to be feelin' when he sees the body of Shard bein' lifted, dead and near frozen from the street? Well, have you?'

* ★ ★

The same thought was troubling Sheriff Hart as he sat patiently in his office waiting for Doc Tucker to finish dressing the flesh wound to his shoulder.

He felt no concern over the death of Spreads Shard — he deserved his miserable fate — but the consequences of it were another matter.

Would there be a violent reaction from Chisholm? Would he seek immediate revenge? Would he order Deloit to kill at will, as the fancy took him? Or might he adopt a more subtle approach? Might he pit his own and Deloit's guile against that of McCallam? Or was it Chater? Hell, just who was the fellow?

'There,' pronounced Doc at last, 'best I can do for now. You got lucky. Another inch to the right and you'd be joinin' Cupcake and Ed — as if I ain't got enough to look to! As it is you'll do. Just don't rate yourself the all-time fast-shootin' lawman. That you most certainly ain't!'

He washed up in the bowl of hot water, buttoned his shirt sleeves and slipped into his coat. 'Time I took a look at the others.' He packed his bag, clicked it shut, and stared hard at the sheriff. 'What you plannin'?' he asked.

'Hard to say,' said Hart, coming to his feet. 'Don't seem a deal to be gained from trying to find McCallam. He'll find us a whole sight easier. On the other hand, there's Chisholm. What the hell is he goin' to do? And when? If he takes it into his head — '

'You reckonin' that this fella McCallam or Chater is really the gun Henry Begine hired? If he is, and if he regards this so-called deal as still bein' valid and there to be fulfilled, well, is he goin' to do just that? Will he set out now to kill Deloit and Chisholm? Some reckon they saw a shadowy figure collectin' Shard's rifle.'

Hart eased himself carefully into his jacket. 'I don't know who the fella is, Doc, but I do know for certain he saved my life back there. Shard was set to pull the trigger point-blank. I stood no chance. Anybody could see that. And I sure as hell knew it. So . . . to be frank, I'd like to shake the fella by the hand and thank him.'

Their conversation faded as both men tensed at the sound of a volley of gunshots then of heavy footfalls thudding along the boardwalk.

The door burst open and a townman, his broad-brimmed hat flopping helplessly across his eyes, his coat tight across layers of sacking scarves, fell into the office as if tossed from the street. 'We got trouble again,' he blurted. 'At the saloon. Chisholm's gone mad. He's shootin' up anythin' that moves. It'll be a bloodbath!'

21

The street had begun to fill again at the sounds of the shooting, ranting and general mayhem from the saloon. Girls screamed; a window was smashed; furniture splintered; empty bottles flew over the batwings to the boardwalk as Chisholm released his booze-sodden anger and stomped round the bar like a bull that had finally slipped its chains.

Moses Fletcher, his barman and a clutch of the girls in various states of undress, were gathered at the back of the saloon as far away, they hoped, from the rampaging Chisholm as they could get.

Deloit lounged at the bar as if merely wiling away the time until something more interesting came his way. He examined his fingers in detail, drew a Colt but only to polish the barrel, spin the chamber and holster the piece again with a flamboyant flourish. Then, between drinks, he watched quietly, a soft smile almost parting his lips as Chisholm continued his passage of destruction. How long, he wondered, before the first killing?

Sheriff Hart, Doc Tucker and the man with the floppy hat had been joined outside the store by Henry Begine. Portly Mann, the hobbling form of Cupcake, a bewildered Ed Birch and a steadily growing crowd of men unable or too scared to sleep.

'This ain't no place for invalids, specially when they're my patients!' scolded Doc, as Cupcake swished his stick through the snow and lent a helping hand to Birch.

'T'ain't doin' us no good sittin' back there at your place, Doc,' wheezed Cupcake. 'Hell, all we can hear is shootin', shoutin', the place bein' smashed to splinters.' He ducked instinctively at another blaze of gunfire, shattering of glass, screams from the girls, the crash of a bottle across the boardwalk. 'Somebody care to hand me a reliable piece, I'll go settle that rat right now. Any offers?'

'You'll just keep yourself clear of the bar,' ordered the sheriff, wrapping himself deep into his coat. 'Same goes for all of you,' he added, raising his voice above the mayhem. 'Appreciate your support and I understand how you feel, but I ain't for givin' Chisholm the chance of a bloodbath.'

'Me neither,' snapped Doc, tightening his grip on his medicine bag. 'I suggest — '

But his words were lost and his voice trailed away at the sight of Chisholm bursting through the batwings, dragging a girl behind him in one hand, a rifle clenched tight in the other.

The men groaned. A younger man sprang forward, only to be pinned where he stood by a burly fellow with a frost-speckled black beard. Sparks and a cloud of smoke billowed and flew from the old-timer's pipe.

'What's he goin' to do now, f'Chris'sake?'

murmured Begine.

'Kill that gal as like as not,' clipped a townman.

'Somebody should blast his guts,' cursed another.

'Give me a piece,' flared Cupcake, thrusting his stick into the snow.

'Hold it!' shouted Hart. 'Don't nobody do anythin'. Clear the street. Get into cover before —'

But no one moved as Chisholm's first shots from the rifle seared across the night sky like shooting stars. His voice ranted behind the blaze. The bar girl fell to her knees. Chisholm dragged her back to her feet. 'Stand, damn you!' he bellowed. He released another blaze of lead, this time lower so that it scorched across the boardwalks opposite and smashed through the store's glass-fronted doors, spinning silver shards in all directions.

'Where the hell's Frank Chater?' mouthed Cupcake, ducking as the shots crashed around him.

'Way out of town if he's got any

215

sense!' piped the old-timer, backing into the deeper cover of the boardwalk.

'Time we woke up round here,' shouted Chisholm behind a flurry of shots and the high-pitched screams of the girl.

'For God's sake somebody do somethin'!' yelled a man in two pairs of trousers with the bottoms bound tight round his ankles.

'You all awake?' bellowed Chisholm again. 'You all here? You all ready to hear what I've got to say?'

The storekeeper groaned and closed his eyes. Portly Mann and Ed Birch exchanged fear-glazed glances. Doc Tucker gulped as he watched first Deloit saunter from the bar, through the 'wings to stand twirling a Colt through his clean, smooth fingers, then Sheriff Hart make his way to the foot of the boardwalk to come face to face with Chisholm.

'I hope you ain't figurin' on interferin' here, Sheriff,' sneered the gunman, swiping the long barrel of the rifle through the air to within inches of Hart's face. 'The law ain't wanted here.' He pulled the terrified bar girl closer to him. 'I'm the law in North Bend! And that's the way it's goin' to stay from here on. You all listenin' up there? Hearin' me loud and clear? Good, then we'll get to the business I got in mind.'

Deloit pushed himself clear of the jamb at the 'wings and glared intently over the faces of the gathering of townsfolk, his fingers dribbling round the butt of the drawn Colt.

The bar girl in Chisholm's grip gritted her teeth and squirmed but to no advantage against the man's hold on her. His fingers simply dug deeper into her cold, shivering flesh.

Moses Fletcher, his face as grey as morning mist, peered over the 'wings, blinked his tired, watery eyes and ran a shaking finger across a twitching nerve in his cheek.

Doc Tucker, Henry Begine and Portly Mann felt suddenly numbed to the bone as if the winter cold had passed through them and frozen them where they stood.

Cupcake rammed his walking stick into the snow and seethed through clenched teeth. Ed Birch's head began to throb. The man with the frost-speckled beard tightened his hold on the youth. The old-timer blew smoke from his pipe and watched it twist and curl on the slow wind from the north.

'The business I have in mind,' continued Chisholm, 'is the matter of who stabbed my good friend and long time partner, Spreads Shard.' He spat into the snow. 'Who, I ask myself? Well, somebody sure as hell did, didn't they? Most of you saw it, watched him fall face-down in the snow there. Weren't booze-bitten fairyland, was it? Weren't no dream. And if the best you can do is tell me that McCallam's back in town, you can save your breath.'

The man's stare deepened and darkened as it ranged over the men and finally came to rest on Sheriff Hart.

'Do you know whose hand was on

that blade, Sheriff?' he asked. 'God knows you were closest. What did you see? Or weren't you for some dumb reason happenin' to be lookin' at that moment?' Chisholm spat again and sneered. 'But mebbe it don't matter none, eh? Mebbe it could've been any one of twenty, thirty men. Any one man. So, we'll do the decent thing and hang just one man. And I ain't fussed which of you it happens to be. In fact, to show you just how fair and decent a fella I really am, I'm goin' to let you choose who gets to hang. That's right — each and every man is goin' to have his say. Can't be fairer than that, can I?'

Chisholm's grin spread like a bad stain across his mouth. He laughed, fired a blaze of shots high into the night, and pulled the half-frozen, shivering girl tighter to him.

'You've got two hours,' shouted Chisholm. 'Just two hours. Till first light. Then we hang the fella you've chosen. So get busy!'

★   ★   ★

'It'd better be me. Goddamnit, I'm an old man. Too old now to recall just how many years I've used up. So I'm your man. Makes sense.'

The old-timer tamped the freshly filled bowl of his pipe, lit it and let a long cloud of smoke drift into the soft glow of the lantern light in Henry Begine's storeroom where Sheriff Hart, Doc Tucker, Portly Mann, Cupcake, the Gopher and a crowd of others had gathered after Chisholm's announcement.

Only Ed Birch and Barney had chosen not to join them and hurried away to the livery. 'You never know, McCallam might show up. Got to rest somewhere, ain't he?' Barney had said, turning his face to the east for a feel of the weather. 'Snow might be passin' on, but hell, it's cold and, I'll wager, so is he.'

Doc Tucker wafted aside the smearing pipe smoke and stepped into the

full spread of the yellow light. 'Appreciate what you're sayin' there, fella, but
there ain't goin' to be nobody *chosen* or
sent in any other way to Chisholm's
hangin' party. And that's standin' as
fact by my reckonin'. Nobody, you
hear? Who the hell does the sonofabitch figure he is? The law, judge, jury
— and now the hangman! Not while
I'm breathin', he ain't. Not in North
Bend. I'd die stoppin' him.'

'Me too,' piped a man.

'And me.'

'I'm with you, Doc.'

'Hang the rat ourselves, I say.'

'So, are we goin' out there fightin'?'
asked Begine above the sudden babble
of voices.

The men fell silent.

'Easy to say, ain't it?' grinned the
old-timer, examining the glow in the
bowl of his pipe. 'We can all talk the
fightin' like nobody's fought before. But
gettin' out there, standin' to it, doin' it
. . . well now, that ain't so easy. Too
right it ain't. There's womenfolk to

221

think to, young uns, homes, property, all the things you've been *fightin'* for all your lives.' The old man lit the pipe again. 'How many are ready to let Chisholm take these from him? What price leavin' a widow to fend best she can, to bring up the youngsters on her own; to mebbe lose her home, everythin', to a man like Chisholm? How many are for *doin'* the fightin'?'

The men stayed silent until Cupcake thudded his stick to the floor. 'Well, mebbe we ain't through yet,' he said, shifting his still painful leg. 'Mebbe Chater or McCallam, whoever he is, will be back. All we need is a fella like him on our side — a real professional — and we've got an edge.'

Sheriff Hart rested his weight on the side of a crate. 'All right, the talkin's over. Ain't nothin' more to be said that ain't been voiced already. Time we got to some practicalities.'

'What's your thinkin', Sheriff?' blinked the man in two pairs of trousers.

'If you're lookin' for volunteers to

fight . . . ' began the youth before a firm hand gripped his arm.

'Mebbe if we all got together, like them dirt-bustin' termites when they get to buildin' and shapin' and doin' . . . ' offered a small, timid man with chattering teeth as he peered over misted spectacles.

Doc raised an arm for quiet. 'Give the sheriff a chance here.'

Hart nodded as he stepped from the shadows. 'All those capable of handlin' a gun, give your name to Doc here. I'm lookin' for the best dozen or so to work directly with me to my orders. If you can't shoot and make it count, stay clear. I'm also askin' Henry here to figure some way of makin' sure we isolate Chisholm in the saloon.'

'What about keepin' an eye on Chisholm and Deloit?' asked Doc.

The sheriff smiled quietly to himself and turned to where the Gopher was lurking in the deeper shadows.

'If you want to stay livin' in this town, mister,' he said carefully, his gaze fixed on the man, 'you're goin' to have to earn the privilege. You ready for that?'

The Gopher nodded anxiously. 'You bet,' he murmured.

'So you stay in the saloon and watch Chisholm's every move. If he or Deloit breaks with routine you report to me. Let Moses Fletcher know what we're doin'. But most of all, you cling to Chisholm at all times. No mistakes, not if you want to stay breathin' . . . '

22

Sheriff Hart gazed over the faces of the group of men gathered in his office and wondered quietly to himself if they were just plain crazy or mule-headed stubborn.

'Six,' said Doc Tucker with a finality that pronounced there would be no more. 'Best shots in town by their own and my reckonin'. All volunteers. You give the orders, they'll see them through.'

'S'right,' smiled a lean rake of a man with a hooded left eye and a greasy growth of stubble. 'You name it, Sheriff, we'll do it. Anythin' to see them scumbags in hell.'

'Same here, Mr Hart,' said a smaller man with a flushed face and lank, greying hair. 'Some of us are mebbe goin' to die in the effort, but we're all for makin' it, damned if we ain't.'

'God willin' there'll be no killin,' said Hart. He glanced quickly at Doc. 'I'm obliged to every one of you for steppin' forward. Together we might, just might, get an edge here.' He glanced at Doc again. 'Though I ain't sure how at this moment.'

'Fate has a way of steppin' in,' added Doc, with a gentle grin.

'Well, who knows, mebbe that fella McCallam will show up again. Sure as hell seems to have a knack of bein' around when he's needed,' said a man keeping watch on the street from the office window. He peered closer. 'But he ain't here now, that's for sure.'

'As far as you can see,' quipped a man sporting a motheaten derby with a bright red feather pinned to the front of it. 'Types like him come and go with the light. Ain't that so, Sheriff? Cupcake reckons — '

'Shall we get to our duties?' suggested Doc.

Sheriff Hart joined the man at the window. 'Two men patrol the street.

226

Keep it clear of anybody who ain't got a right to be there. Last thing we want is an audience. Try to keep as many folk as possible confined to their homes, specially them hot-blooded youths with fancy ideas of what they can do with a gun.

'Cupcake, Ed Birch and Barney are goin' about livery business. One of you fellas get up there to keep a watch on who might be tryin' to leave. I ain't expectin' too many ridin' in! I want a couple of men positioned back of the saloon. That's five of you. One man stays here along of Doc. As for myself, I'll be wherever I figure I'm needed.'

'And what happens come first light when Chisholm gets to lookin' for the fella to hang?' asked the man with the hooded eye.

'Now that,' said Doc, 'is where fate might step in.'

★ ★ ★

It was fate and its fickle moods that was haunting Henry Begine. Fate that had

227

brought Chisholm and his sidekicks to North Bend; fate that had led to the deal struck with Frank Chater and finally brought him to town, only for fate to twist and turn again and reduce the gunman to little more than a man in hiding. If, in fact, he was Chater.

So what had fate in store, he wondered, watching from the board-walk as Portly Mann and a group of men went about securing what they could of the town's business properties? More killing, more bodies and misery as the leftovers of North Bend crumbled under Chisholm's tyranny?

He shivered and hugged himself deeper into his coat. He was living in dread of the first light lifting in the east, of Chisholm stepping out of the saloon bar to prepare for a hanging, of the death of the first man — or woman, come to that — who stood to defy him.

Could fate be that cruel?

It could, he thought, his gaze shifting to follow the two men leaving the sheriff's office to take up street patrol.

Anything might happen; a careless word, a wrong move, a display of bravado by some mouthy youth, the reappearance of McCallam as most folk now seemed to know him. How long was Chater going to keep up that pretence, he pondered? Was it serving any purpose?

He pulled at his coat again and stamped his feet for warmth against the creeping cold. Damn the weather, he cursed inwardly. Damn Chisholm. Damn the town! How would it ever get back to being as it was?

His thoughts drifted at the sight of Barney hurrying best he could through the snow from the livery, his black bulk moving across the frozen street like some freak shadow.

Henry moved down the boardwalk to meet him. 'Hey, what's the hurry, Barney?' he asked, as the fellow trudged closer.

'Riders,' huffed Barney, his breath swirling round his head. 'Comin' in from the east. We figure two of 'em. Be here we reckon, in twenty minutes or so. Best let the sheriff know. He in his office?'

Henry nodded, a frown deepening across his brow. 'Riders?' he murmured vaguely. 'At this hour in these conditions? Who in hell would want to be ridin' anywhere, let alone to North Bend in this weather?'

Fate, he thought, was never satisfied.

★　★　★

They had trimmed the single lantern to the dimmest glow that lay on the snow like a smeared, dissolving stain. The wind was freshening again, the early light gathering in grey sprawled streaks behind the retreating night. The cold crept about looking to make mischief where clothes were too loose or too thin to protect. But none of the dozen or so men gathered at the livery seemed to notice it. They had more pressing concerns clearing the horizon in the shape of the riders set on a course for North Bend.

'Ain't in no doubt where they're headin',' said the old-timer through a twist of smoke from his freshly lit pipe.

'Must've been ridin' best part of the night,' said Portly Mann, wiping the backs of his hands across his eyes as he strained for a clearer view. 'Can't make 'em out at this distance. Still too far away.'

'Definitely two,' murmured Henry Begine.

'Fair lookin' horses they've got there,' added Barney.

Cupcake scratched his chin. 'I'd figure for them ridin' the same trail as myself and Chater. From the south. I'd wager they cleared the forest noon yesterday.'

'Be more than ready to rest up time they get here,' said the man wearing two pairs of trousers.

'But why here?' pondered Doc Tucker. 'Why North Bend?'

'Ain't no other place, Doc,' countered Cupcake. 'You clear that forest and turn north, you got only one choice: North Bend or nothin'. And nothin' don't figure when winter's got a grip.'

Doc mused thoughtfully for a moment. 'Hm,' he murmured softly. 'So mebbe them fellas out there set out with North Bend in mind.' He reflected again, catching Sheriff Hart's quick glance. 'I wonder why?'

Portly Mann cleared his throat carefully as he tightened his shredded woollen scarf. 'Could be, o' course, that they're friends of Chisholm. Mebbe they're his men. Mebbe he's known all along they'd be ridin' in.' He swallowed, conscious of the dark looks closing in on him.

'You seriously reckon that?' said Henry Begine. 'You figure for Chisholm arrangin' for others to join him? Sorry, I don't. No, that ain't Chisholm. He's only for himself.'

The old-timer watched a smear of pipe smoke lose itself on the growing light. 'They're carryin' some iron,' he said quietly, his eyes narrowing. 'See that fella leadin', he's tacked up with double rifle scabbards. Same goes for his partner.'

'I see 'em,' confirmed Hart, pulling his coat across his body.

'You want I should bring up more guns, Sheriff?' asked a spotty-faced youth with a crop of cold sores round his lips. 'There's fellas back there willin' enough.'

'No more guns,' said Hart. 'Just keep a close eye on that saloon bar. Last thing we want here is a reception committee controlled by Chisholm. Tell Moses to open a bottle of his best or somethin'.'

The youth nodded and skidded away through the snow.

'Mebbe I'll brew up a fresh pot of coffee,' said Barney, picking his way back to the smoking forge.

'Good thinkin',' muttered the old-timer. He drew heavily on his pipe. 'Meantime ... yeah, meantime I'm figurin' them riders there ain't drifters ironed up like that. Then there's their hats.'

'Hats?' frowned Doc. 'What's hats got to do with it?'

The old-timer blew the pipe smoke high across the still freshening wind. 'Eastern mould, ain't they? Shaped up city style. Fancy-dandy, I'd reckon. Fellas more used to cut-glass than tin. Not your average North Bend types, eh, Sheriff?'

Sheriff Hart merely grunted quietly and disregarded the chill groping icily along his spine.

23

The riders reined their mounts out of the high-stepping trot that had cleared the deeper snow and slowed them to a shuffling walk once they had the livery and the town men in clear view. Then, like perched hawks, they waited.

Doc Tucker nudged his medicine bag into Sheriff Hart's thigh. 'He was right,' he murmured. 'It's like the old fella said, they ain't no drifters. Nothin' like.'

'You gentlemen cut the trail from the south?' asked Cupcake, his gaze tightening its concentration on the riders' faces. 'Tough goin' this time of the year.'

The taller, leaner of the men, with ice-blue eyes, a fresh snow-winds' tan darkening his clean-shaven face, tipped the brim of his grey, shaped hat and smiled. 'You may say that with certainty, sir. It is indeed a mean winter. Is it always this cold?' he asked politely, in a pitched, polished voice.

'Gets colder,' quipped the old-timer, his pipe smoke swirling excitedly.

The second rider, a slightly stockier version of his partner, but with equally ice-blue eyes and a rich tan colouring his smooth skin, adjusted a niftily tied bandanna at his throat and rubbed his gloved hands together for warmth. 'I don't think I've ever seen a more welcomin' sight than the forge I see there,' he grinned. 'Wouldn't you say so, Mr Bridge?'

'Most definitely, Mr Ford,' replied his companion, his smile still lingering. 'And would I be mistaken, or is that the sublime aroma of coffee headin' my way?'

'You are not at all mistaken, Mr Bridge. Coffee — fresh as the balm of Heaven.'

'Dudes!' hissed the old-timer under his breath.

'You fellas won't be for passin' through?' said the sheriff.

'Ah, a man of the law,' smiled the man in the grey hat, lifting it in acknowledgement. 'Allow me to introduce ourselves. I am Mr Ford, at your service, sir, and my companion, fellow traveller and long-time partner in business here, is Mr Bridge.' He posed a bow from his seat in the saddle. 'Delighted to make your acquaintance and to have reached your most welcomin' town.' His smile ranged over the faces watching him in silence. 'This is North Bend, I take it?'

'You got it, mister,' said Doc, stepping forward. 'Name's Tucker. I'm the physician hereabouts, and these fellas are the good townsfolk of North Bend. You were headin' our way?'

'Oh, most certainly,' said the man introduced as Mr Bridge. 'We left Williamsville some time back with the sole intention of reaching North Bend.'

'Why?' snapped the sheriff. 'Why North Bend? Hell, we ain't nothin' to speak of. Hardly make it onto the map.'

'Well, of course, there are reasons,'

said Ford, tightening the reins as his mount shifted and pawed uncomfortably. 'We have, you might say, a purpose.'

'And what might that be exactly?' asked Henry Begine.

The riders exchanged glances as if in silent confirmation of agreement.

'We happen,' said Ford, 'to be looking for somebody.'

'To be in search of him really for his own good,' added Bridge immediately. 'Before anythin' . . . unfortunate . . . might befall him,' he added hurriedly, a smile adding sparkle to his ice-blue stare.

'And who might this fella be?' frowned Hart, conscious of the cold sting across his back.

'Ah,' said Ford, raising an arm, 'he might, you see, be anybody. By which I mean to say he might be travellin' incognito.' He paused a moment, watching the faces turned on him. 'Under another name. Because — '

'Because,' broke in Bridge, 'he is what is known as on the run.'

'An escaped prisoner,' said Ford.

'Out of the penitentiary at Williamsville,' added his partner.

Ford's expression darkened. 'A quite notorious outlaw, serving sentence on a number of counts.'

'He shot a senior guard among others in pursuit of him,' said Bridge. 'We found the bodies and deduced that our man was heading north. And north to us gentlemen, means only one thing: North Bend.'

'Quite so,' smiled Ford. 'The tracks in parts were clear enough. There was no doubtin' the destination was to be the town of North Bend. So here we are!'

'Had any strangers through lately?' asked Bridge.

'Town gets its fair share same as any other place,' said the sheriff before any of the men could speak. 'I ain't fussed none so long as they keep their noses clean and ain't for makin' trouble. But in winter . . . well, that's different, ain't it? I mean, folk don't get to travellin', do they? Tend to stay wherever they're holed up.'

Bridge's gaze deepened. 'So there have been no strangers through; no fella looking as though he might be in a hurry to be somewhere else?'

'What's your interest?' said Hart, his tone hardening.

Doc Tucker tightened his grip on his bag. The old-timer released a swirl of smoke and narrowed his gaze. Henry Begine felt a trickle of cold sweat easing down his spine. Cupcake held his stick firm and steady in the snow.

'You fellas jail guards?' muttered a youth, swallowing noisily.

Ford's smile took a while to break. 'Well, not exactly,' he began. 'Which is to say not officially, although in a manner of speakin' we are representin' — '

'This fella on the run, this escaped prisoner, got a name?' blurted Begine, unable now to control his anxiety and wincing as the cold sweat seeped below his belt line.

'Might have a whole string of them by this time,' said Bridge. 'Changes them, you see, to suit the circumstances in which he finds himself.'

Ford adjusted the set of his hat and leaned forward in the saddle as the steam rose like a veil from his mount. 'We know him as McCallam. That's his real name.'

'John McCallam,' added Bridge with a gaze that missed nothing of the reactions on the faces of the men staring at him.

* * *

'So has Frank Chater taken the name McCallam; or is McCallam — the real John McCallam who's on the run out of the pen at Williamsville — assumin' the name Chater as a cover? Who in the name of sanity, is who?'

Cupcake leaned on his stick, blinked across the grey, sullen light of the livery stables and let his tired shoulders slump under the weight of his heavy coat.

241

Henry Begine paced into the shadows, turned and came back to the open doors where the men were gathered. 'But if McCallam is posin' as Chater, then where's the real Chater? And how come McCallam — if that's who he is — came to be wearin' the exact same clothes as Chater?'

'Mebbe Chater's dead,' said Portly Mann.

'You sayin' as how McCallam stole a dead man's clothes?' frowned Ed Birch. 'Stripped a stiff body and stepped into the fella's pants and coat?'

'It's possible,' murmured the storekeeper, his head aching with questions.

'Don't really matter, does it?' grunted the old-timer. 'Chater, McCallam, whoever, he's gettin' at Chisholm and Deloit. Ain't no escapin' that for a fact. The fella kills, and makes a darn good job of it.' He examined the unlit bowl of his dusty pipe. 'But that ain't for matterin' a deal neither. The real problem's them two fellas, the smooth-tongued Eastern types callin' themselves

Mr Bridge and Mr Ford. Bah, I ain't heard nothin' so dude-janglin' in my life! I'll tell you what they are, they're bounty hunters through to the marrow. That's what they are!'

'And if they are,' added Doc, gazing into the snow-trapped empty street, 'Chisholm's goin' to welcome them with open arms. They'll be the guns to take out the problem of McCallam.'

'Where are they now?' asked the man with the bushy beard.

'The saloon,' murmured Doc, 'doin' a deal with Chisholm by now I'd reckon.'

'And McCallam — where's he?' asked Barney.

No one answered. Eyes turned to the street, to the light struggling for its hold on the day, the faint lantern glow at the Saddles saloon in an otherwise silent, sleeping sweep of snow marked only by scuffed footfalls and the tracks of a loping dog.

Somewhere out there a man was in hiding, fighting to cling on to life and perhaps make another desperate bid for freedom.

★   ★   ★

'We have a deal, gentlemen,' beamed Royce Chisholm, gesturing through the thickening, smoke-filled gloom of the saloon to the barman for a fresh bottle.

He waited until the bottle was opened and on the table then poured four stiff measures to clean glasses. 'To the killin' of John McCallam,' he beamed again, leading the toast. 'And may it come fast!'

Deloit, standing at Chisholm's side, raised his glass and downed the measure in a single, lip-smacking gulp. He belched loudly and spat into the nearest spittoon. 'May he rot in hell!' he muttered.

'Amen to that, eh, gentlemen?' echoed Chisholm, settling his dark gaze on Ford and Bridge where they stood some feet from the table, their backs to the 'wings.

Ford glanced quickly at Bridge then

244

passed the measure of whiskey under his nose once, twice, before sampling the drink with the merest sip. His companion did likewise, sampling the drink with his eyes closed.

'Don't suppose you Eastern boys rate the local varnish, that it?' grinned Chisholm, refilling his glass. 'Well, don't figure for you havin' to suffer it long. We'll get this business cleared up in no time. What d'you say, Deloit? What do you figure — a day, half of a day, mebbe only a matter of a coupla hours, eh?'

Deloit remained silent, his gaze fixed and steady on Ford and Bridge.

'Let me be sure of the detail of the *deal* you are proposin',' said Bridge in his carefully delivered and polished tone. 'You — yourself and Mr Deloit — will, as you say, *deliver* the man McCallam to within reach of our guns to do with as we please: shoot outright, or take prisoner alive as we see fit. Is that the essence of the *deal*, Mr Chisholm?'

'You got it, Mr Bridge,' grinned Chisholm, gesturing with his half-empty glass. 'Top and bottom of it. No frills, no fancies.' He leaned forward across the table. 'And we don't want a cent of the bounty money you'll collect back at Williamsville. Not a single cent, gentlemen.' He relaxed again, finished the drink and slid the glass across the table to come to rest at the side of the bottle as if it belonged there.

Ford cleared his throat politely behind a fisted hand. 'Why?' he asked softly. 'Why no share of the bounty money to you?'

'Ah,' said Chisholm, bustling unsteadily to his feet, 'the answer to that is simple enough, my friends.' He gazed round the bar, at the grey, worn faces of Moses Fletcher and his barman, at the huddle of bar girls keeping their distance in the shadows; the hand-twisting, sniffling, shifty-eyed Gopher, and the sleeping town drunk slumped alone at a drink-stained table. 'I already have my bounty,' smiled Chisholm, raising his arms. 'I have this — the town. It's all mine, gentlemen, every last stick of it, every last plank and nail of everythin' standin'. Plus, I should add, every last soul livin' here, even that numbskull sheriff.' He laughed until he was dribbling. 'This place — and them gals! Go on, help yourselves. Have them on me!'

Ford gave the girls an airy, disdainful glance. 'Thank you, but not our types, eh, Mr Bridge?'

'Most definitely not our types, Mr Ford,' agreed Bridge.

'Suit yourselves,' rumbled Chisholm, stepping to the bar. He paused a moment, his face darkening to his thoughts. 'I got only one concern, one burr burnin' in my boot: McCallam is a real pain right now. I want him dead and out of *my* town. You fellas do that for me and I'll have all the bounty I'll ever need — '

The explosion, when it came, blew almost half the main street to flying timbers and shattered glass within seconds.

24

North Bend shuddered as if rocked by a vicious earthquake, its very bones threatening to crush under the sheer force of the blast.

The centre of it, so far as anyone could reckon in those nerve-shattering first minutes, was at the rear of Henry Begine's mercantile, where only hours before the town men had gathered with the Gopher and Sheriff Hart. Now it was simply a flattened area, littered with the splinters of ripped timbers, the smashed remains of stores, the shreds of clothing and blankets. The main store building had been blown clean into the street, taking the goods area, the first floor and Begine's private quarters with it, spewing the contents across the snow like handfuls of some surreal confetti.

The store's front doors lay among the

devastation almost unscathed as if waiting for a hand to push them open. The candy jar and biscuit barrel treats were scattered among pick handles, brooms, broken boxes, boots, ropes, hammers, nails, hoes and, blackened beyond recognition, a once bright blue bonnet.

The neighbouring buildings to both left and right, had been flattened; the buildings beyond them similarly destroyed, so that virtually one whole length of the street was no more. Only a short stretch of boardwalk remained in place; coming from nowhere, going nowhere.

Buildings on the opposite side of the street had suffered comparatively minor damage; broken windows, doors ripped from their hinges, roofs pierced, walls chipped and bruised, a rocker thrown high to land impaled on a picket fence, a hitching rail felled and flattened as if in the path of a stampede.

But in all the chaos, mayhem and destruction there had been no deaths and only minor injuries to arms and legs. Far more folk fell to the trauma of shock and bewilderment, particularly those who had seen property collapse before their eyes.

'What the hell happened?' shouted a man, standing marooned in the middle of the street, smoke, dust and dirt swirling round him.

'Dynamite,' yelled another. 'Begine had a whole stash of it out back.'

'Who primed it, f'Chris'sake?'

But there were no answers offered readily, though most, if they were honest, would have figured for the culprit being McCallam.

'Go where you're needed, Doc,' said Sheriff Hart, emerging grey and dusty from his debris-scarred office. He paused on the pitted boardwalk for a moment, trying to take in the devastation.

'Hell on earth,' murmured Doc, as if to speak the sheriff's thoughts. He spat dirt from his parched mouth, and blinked. 'Lucky there ain't a fire — yet.' He spat again. 'You reckon for this bein' McCallam's way of remindin' us he's still around?'

'One helluva reminder!' muttered Hart, watching carefully as the street began to fill. 'Best take a look at Henry. He's goin' to need you.'

'And you? Where you goin' to be? If McCallam decides — '

'Chisholm and them new-found friends of his will be bristlin'. I'm reckonin' on the lead startin' to fly in about — '

And then it did.

★   ★   ★

The first shots blazed from the boardwalk fronting the saloon, roared like spits of flame through the still billowing, swirling smoke of the explosion to climb high into the morning light.

And with them came a stream of growled abuse and curses from the dripping mouth of Royce Chisholm as he crashed through the batwings in a

251

crunch of body and limbs to straddle the board like a crazed black bear.

'Who the hell's blowin' up my town?' he bellowed. '*My town*. You hear that? My town!'

He blazed another shot, fumbled the Colt through his fingers on the recoil and was close to losing his grip on the piece when the man in two pairs of trousers, his eyes alight, his face a muddle of sweat, dust, dirt and grime, his hands tight on a rifle carried across his front, sloshed his way through the snow and debris to stand within yards of him.

'That's it, Chisholm,' he shouted, his voice cracking on his nerve. 'End of the line. We've had enough. All of us. Every last man. You and your kind ain't fit to stay breathin'. You hear me . . . '

His voice stumbled on, lifting and falling, cracking and threatening to die in a hiss as the townsfolk gathered, some behind him standing where they could balance in the scattered destruction, some at a safer distance peering through the still drifting curtain of smoke.

'Darn fool,' muttered Portly Mann, slipping and sliding through a patch of melting snow where the wintry sun struck it.

'Get himself killed sure as fate,' murmured the old-timer, his pipe smoke clamouring against the smoke cloud.

Barney and Ed Birch turned away to calm spooked horses.

Cupcake smashed his stick against a splintered plank and cursed. Then he spat and hit the plank again. An old woman, oblivious to the activity, salvaged a crushed bonnet from beneath a broken crate and patted the twisted ribbons into shape.

A young boy sporting an oversized hat that almost covered his eyes, dared to throw a snowball in the direction of the saloon.

Doc Tucker tightened his grip on Sheriff Hart's arm and urged him to go easy. 'Too many guns, Jess. A whole sight too many.'

The sheriff pulled away. 'What the hell does the fool think he's doin'?'

But he was already too late to make a positive move as a gun blazed, this time from the man in the street.

His aim had been wild. He had screwed his eyes tight through the roar, gritted his teeth and felt his stomach drop to his bowel like a sliver of ice. When he summoned the courage to open his eyes he saw Chisholm still standing, still wearing that half-crazed grin, the Colt firm in his grip again.

But now Deloit was at his side, twin guns levelled, steady, waiting to strike like roused rattlers.

The man in the street took a stumbled step back, shuddered, stared open-mouthed. He gulped on a sudden grittiness deep in his throat. Why was the street beginning to spin? Why were there so many faces; so many eyes watching him? Why was there so much silence?

The guns in Deloit's hands seemed

to grow until he thought he would be sucked into their barrels. Was this death? Was this how it felt . . . a spinning street, faces, eyes, gun barrels, silence?

Another blaze of gunfire shook the man into losing his balance. His legs melted; he fell into the snow and dirt like thrown trash, but he sensed an icy cold between his fingers, across his spine. No, damnit, he was not dead! He was alive.

He began to struggle upright again. 'Stay down, f'Chris'sake!' yelled a voice from somewhere in the chaos of destruction behind him. He fell back instinctively, gunfire screaming and blazing above him, around him, spitting through the snow and slush like white-hot pokers hissing into water. But not *at* him. The shots were not aimed at him. They came from the right, among the debris of Henry Begine's store.

He heard Chisholm curse; the batwings creak and swing on their tired hinges; a bar girl scream; glass smashing; more yells and shouts, more screams. And then a lone voice raised above the others. Cupcake's voice, repeating the same two words time and time again:

'Deloit's down! Deloit's down!'

'He's right,' said Doc at Sheriff Hart's side. 'Down — and he ain't movin'.'

Hart narrowed his gaze to scan the street debris. It had been McCallam's gun blazing from wherever he had holed himself in cover; his shots that had ripped first into Deloit's arm forcing him to drop one of his twin Colts, then without mercy blazed three fast shots into his chest and gut.

Chisholm had scrambled away, crashed through the batwings and into the bar. But what now? 'Keep folk as far away from the saloon as you can, Doc,' said Hart, adjusting the set of his gunbelt. 'I'm goin' in there. Back door if I can.'

'Don't you reckon — ?' But Doc's anxious protest fell on deaf ears as the sheriff was lost almost instantly in the smoke-clouded air and piled clutters of debris.

He weaved his way quickly towards the rear of the saloon and passed like a shadow into the scattered barrels, crates and boxes that cluttered it and was within a dozen steps of the door that led to the bar's storeroom, when it opened and Maisie Peach tumbled out.

'Am I glad to see you,' she gasped, falling into his arms with a shudder that seemed to rack her whole body. 'I was on my way to find you. Get some help. Them slick-lipped bounty hunters who didn't want to be within a sniff of us girls an hour ago, have gotten to changin' their minds. Now they're all over us — and not very decent with it.'

'Where's Chisholm?' asked the sheriff.

'Back in the bar and lookin' like he's seen a ghost now that Deloit ain't standin' to him. If you're goin' to get him, Mr Hart, now's the time for sure.' Maisie brushed her hair from her face. 'You goin' in there?'

Hart nodded. 'You seen anythin' of that fella McCallam?'

Maisie shook her head. 'But it must've been him that shot Deloit,' she said, wincing at the throb of a bruise across her neck. 'Ain't nobody in North Bend to my knowledge who can handle a Winchester like that at a distance.' She tossed her hair again. 'If you're goin' in there, I'm comin' with you.'

The storeroom was in near total darkness save for the thin spread of light that crept from beneath the door to the bar. Hart blinked, watched the light dim and flare as bodies passed across it. He put a finger to his lips to signal maximum quiet and crept softly across the dusty floor to the side of the door.

A board creaked on the approach of a heavier footfall. A girl stifled a half scream and began to sob. Maisie tensed, her lips setting to a tight line as she bit back her anger. Hart concentrated to catch Chisholm's sudden bout of ranting between hefty belches.

'That's him . . . that's your man, all

right,' he groaned. 'Heard that Win-chester, didn't you? Deloit sure as hell did! He heard it — and felt it, damn McCallam's eyes.' He belched, spat, clinked the neck of a bottle across the rim of a glass. 'So what you fellas goin' to do, eh? How do a couple of cool-talkin' bounty hunters, with a big catch almost in their sights, set about haulin' their fella in?'

Chisholm began to titter, then to laugh from deep within his gut; a spluttering spitting, that left him dribbling like a babe. Maisie crept closer, strips of her torn dress trailing behind her like shredded wings.

'Well, Mr Ford, Mr Bridge? I'm listenin',' spluttered Chisholm. 'What you goin' to do? Your man's here. Somewhere out there. Mebbe he's waitin' on you . . . lurkin' there . . . prowlin' about . . . watchin' . . . fin-gers itchy to get that Winchester blazin' again, eh? Blazin' like there was never goin' to be no tomorrow. Just like that — '

'You have a problem here. It's for you to settle. We're leaving' snapped Ford in a firm, commanding tone.

Hart gulped, his eyes blinking on the darkness of the storeroom. He felt Maisie's fingers clench under the weight of his hand. He could imagine the look on Chisholm's face, the sudden beading of a soft, sticky sweat across his brow.

He squeezed her hand, signalled again for silence, released himself in a slow step forward and laid his fingers on the handle of the door. Dare he risk opening it? Supposing it squeaked. If Chisholm or the bounty hunters sensed another presence would their guns rage regardless of targets?

He rested his fingers easy, caught the sharp, anxious warmth of Maisie's breath on his neck, and listened to the measured steps of Ford and Bridge as they walked to the batwings.

25

Sheriff Hart cursed quietly to himself as his fingers tightened on the handle and eased the door open the vital chink that gave him a view of the bar.

Chisholm was standing uncertainly behind his table, a bottle of whiskey and glass in front of him, one hand hovering over the butt of his holstered Colt, his glare fierce, burning like flame on the backs of Ford and Bridge.

The Gopher cowered a few yards away in the smokehazed shadow, his eyes flicking frantically from Chisholm to the bounty hunters, back again, until it seemed they would roll from their sockets.

A handful of townmen were gathered at the far end of the bar, none of them daring to speak, not a movement between them, save for the anxiety in their flickering glances, anywhere that avoided Chisholm's gaze.

Moses Fletcher stood behind the bar, as if in defiance of its ownership, his hands shaking, the colour draining from his face to leave a grey mask. The bar girls had clustered at the foot of the stairs where they shivered and comforted each other in soft whispers through stifled sobs.

'Nobody turns his back on me,' ranted Chisholm, sweeping aside the bottle and glass to a shattered mass across the floor. 'You hear me there, you scumbags?'

The bounty hunters halted, turned and fixed their cold stares on the swaying, sweating bulk addressing them.

'Do we hear him, Mr Ford?' asked Bridge.

'I think we do, Mr Bridge,' replied his partner through a soft grin.

'In which case, Mr Ford . . . '

'In which case, Mr Bridge . . . '

A cold chill surged down Hart's spine as drawn guns raged. Maisie clung to him in a petrified shudder. The

Gopher fell back to the wall. Moses Fletcher gripped the bar as if to hold it down. The bar girls sank to their knees.

The gunsmoke from the bounty-hunters' shots hung like a dark breath, clearing slowly on the sight of Chisholm clinging desperately to the table, his eyes wide, fixed, then rolling as the heat of the blazed lead deepened in his gut.

Ford began to smile while he watched Chisholm try to tighten his grip on the table, lose it and slide almost gently, like a carefully lowered weight, to the floor. Splinters of the broken bottle crushed under his body.

'A long time dyin', wouldn't you say. Mr Ford?' said Bridge.

'Tiresomely long, Mr Bridge,' sighed Ford. 'But quite dead now, I believe.' He paused, nodded to his partner, then moved quickly to the storeroom door and pulled it free of Hart's grip. 'Ah, as we suspected, Mr Bridge, we have an audience.' His smile broadened. 'You can come out now, Sheriff.'

Hart and Maisie blinked on the brighter light as they stepped into the bar. Moses Fletcher stiffened again, the group of townmen edged deeper into the shadows; the Gopher dusted himself down. Maisie gestured to the cowering girls to stay where they were.

'What game are you fellas playin' here?' croaked Hart.

'Well, now, Sheriff,' began Ford, 'I would've thought that fairly obvious. However . . . Mr Bridge and myself have figured that in our line of business, the takin', dead or alive, of Royce Chisholm and his sidekicks infinitely more profitable than wastin' time and more energy, in these conditions, on the possibility of McCallam showin' himself, even though we know he's here. And we further thought, in the interests of the well-bein' of the town, that you and the good folk here would much prefer Chisholm dead.'

He smiled as his gaze shifted to the sprawled, lifeless body behind the table. 'So much easier and far less trouble to transport in these wintry conditions, wouldn't you agree?' He turned to his partner. 'Have I covered the relevant points, Mr Bridge?'

'Most certainly, Mr Ford,' said Bridge, helping himself to the drink willingly poured by Moses Fletcher. 'Your health, Sheriff,' he gestured, raising the glass. 'And to North Bend,' he added, turning to toast the gathering of men making their slow, careful way through the batwings to the bar.

'My sentiments exactly, Mr Bridge,' smiled Ford. 'I am sure these long-sufferin' folk are mightily relieved to be rid of such unfortunate characters.'

'You can say that again!' piped an eager youth, making his way to the shivering bar girls.

'Now hold on there a minute,' called Sheriff Hart, stepping forward as the bar began to fill, heads craning for a sight of Chisholm's body now being examined by Doc Tucker. 'Let me get this straight: you fellas intend cartin' the bodies of Chisholm, Deloit and

Shard to — where exactly?'

'To Williamsville, where I feel sure the territorial marshal will be more than happy to see us,' said Ford.

'A fair trek, but we shall hope for improvin' weather,' nodded Bridge. 'And we shall not have extra mouths to feed and water!'

'Or keep warm!' quipped the old-timer, lighting his pipe in a flurry of flame.

'Take the scum, I say,' clipped the man with the bushy beard.

'He's right,' added the man in two pairs of trousers. 'Just get 'em out of our town.'

'It's the best deal I've heard in weeks,' said Portly Mann. 'We set these fellas up best we can with supplies and extra horses for the bodies, and that's the last we ever see of Chisholm. How about that, folks? Ain't that a good deal?'

The men voiced their agreement.

'Not so fast,' urged Henry Begine, raising his arms as he stepped to the centre of the bar. 'There's the question of McCallam? What about him? We sure as hell owe the fella. Remember he took out Spreads Shard and Deloit.'

'You bet he did,' said Cupcake, joining the storekeeper. 'And he saved my life. Don't forget that. I'm not likely to!'

'Where is he now?' asked Begine. 'Anybody seen him?'

'Nobody ever sees McCallam,' said the old-timer, releasing a cloud of smoke from his glowing pipe.

'Nor are they likely to,' murmured Doc stepping away from the dead body. 'His work here is done. Time he moved on, I'd reckon. Whoever he is, whatever he might have done. I ain't fussed. As far as I'm concerned, he saved the life of North Bend. Its life and its soul.'

He swung round to face Bridge and Ford. 'And if you fellas so much as breathe the name McCallam anywhere, anytime, I swear to God we'll see you perish in hell. No question. No messin'. No idle threat. You ain't never seen or heard of McCallam. That's the deal.'

'The only deal, if you want to leave this town still breathin',' added Sheriff Hart as the room fell silent and the folk of North Bend waited for an answer.

Five minutes later they had it.

★　★　★

John McCallam cleared the last of the snowline an hour after sun-up on a trail heading due north.

Only then did he take a deep breath, pat the mare's neck and flick his fingers over her ears as she tossed her head and snorted her own acknowledgement to survival. They had made it, beaten the odds of slipping clear of North Bend unnoticed and come this far through the packed ice and snow and biting north-easterly winds.

'You bet!' he murmured, dropping the reins to sit easy in the saddle, relishing for the first time in two days the need not to look behind him.

Even so, he did.

No sign of being followed; no hint that the bounty hunters had continued to track him. Maybe they had settled instead for the prize of Royce Chisholm and his sidekicks. He relaxed again as his thoughts cleared from the jumbled twists and turns of events since finding the cabin, the body of Frank Chater, the subsequent meeting with Cupcake and the journey to North Bend.

Had it all really happened following his escape from the penitentiary at Williamsville: the shootings, the battle to survive the harshness of the weather, the blowing up of half the town, the arrival of the bounty hunters? Or would he wake as if from some long dream to find himself back in the cabin figuring the possibilities of assuming a dead man's identity?

He shrugged himself deeper into the rags and scarves that passed for the moment for clothes and adjusted the battered hat he had retrieved before the explosion. Maybe he should have

269

stayed, he mused, apologized for the destruction, waited to help the likes of Henry Begine, Portly Mann, Moses Fletcher, Maisie Peach, Doc Tucker, Ed Birch, Barney, the sheriff, to rebuild and settle the town again as it was meant to be.

Or maybe he had best hold to the trail heading north and trust that a future lay somewhere along the horizon. As to who he was ... Frank Chater, John McCallam ... he could be anyone he chose to be. Who could say, there might be another cabin coming up, another chance to be a man with a new name? Or maybe he would ride by without a second glance.

He clicked his tongue for the mare to trot on.

We do hope that you have enjoyed reading this large print book.

Did you know that all of our titles are available for purchase?

We publish a wide range of high quality large print books including:
Romances, Mysteries, Classics
General Fiction
Non Fiction and Westerns

Special interest titles available in large print are:
The Little Oxford Dictionary
Music Book, Song Book
Hymn Book, Service Book

Also available from us courtesy of Oxford University Press:
Young Readers' Dictionary
(large print edition)
Young Readers' Thesaurus
(large print edition)

For further information or a free brochure, please contact us at:
Ulverscroft Large Print Books Ltd.,
The Green, Bradgate Road, Anstey,
Leicester, LE7 7FU, England.
Tel: (00 44) **0116 236 4325**
Fax: (00 44) **0116 234 0205**

Other titles in the
Linford Western Library:

HELL'S COURTYARD

Cobra Sunman

Indian Territory, popularly called
Hell's Courtyard, was where bad
men fled to escape the law. Buck
Rogan, a deputy marshal hunting
the killer Jed Calder, found the trail
leading into Hell's Courtyard and
went after his quarry, finding every
man's hand against him. Rogan was
also searching for the hideout of Jake
Yaris, an outlaw running most of
the lawlessness directed at Kansas
and Arkansas. Single-minded and
capable, Rogan would fight the bad
men to the last desperate shot.